The Record Prophets is Matthew Seery's debut novel. After teaching English and critiquing high school students' papers for nearly a decade, he decided to finally take his own advice and write this book. When he isn't corrupting the minds of the youth, he enjoys his time with his beautiful wife and two sons in their home on the south shore of Long Island, New York.

THE
RECORD
PROPHETS

MATTHEW SEERY

SilverWood

Published in 2015 by SilverWood Books

SilverWood Books Ltd
30 Queen Charlotte Street, Bristol, BS1 4HJ
www.silverwoodbooks.co.uk

ISBN 978-1-78132-365-6 (paperback)
ISBN 978-1-78132-366-3 (ebook)

British Library Cataloguing in Publication Data
A CIP catalogue record for this book is available from
the British Library

Set in Bembo by SilverWood Books
Printed on responsibly sourced paper

Dedication

I dedicate this book to my beautiful wife, Christine, who supported me through every draft and revision. I cannot thank Helen Hart, Bronwen Wotton, and the rest of the SilverWood team enough for their help in making this dream come true. A special thanks to Stephanie Koch and Christi Dionis for your edits, notes, and help. Finally I'd like to thank my financial backers. This book is as much yours as it is mine.

Debby and Jim Seery	Cheryl Curcio
Trisha Rossi	Angela Guertin
Mike Berretta	Kathy Berntson
John and Kathy Petretti	Neil and Mary Talbot
Jenny Zaun	Chris Moore
Rebecca and Matthew Rhine	Rachel Siegel
Courtney Foley	Laura Press
Naresh Sawlani	Sarah Cookinham
Bryn Elliott	Karen O'Neill
Stephanie Koch	Jim Ross
Brendan Fredette	Greg Litcher
Eric Ferraro	Jill and David Trovillion
James Seery	Danielle Amero
Martha Seery	Alyssa Berntson

Joanne Seery

Dan Buscetta

Elizabeth A. Saetta

Ryan O'Rourke

Maura McCue

Alison Haun

Dawn Johnson

Marge Debowy

Sergei Ruber

Part One

Resurrecting Nate Poulfry

I

"You're not listening, and I'm not going to tell you what you want to hear, so let me reiterate it for you one more time: you haven't had it in years and you're never going to have it again," said Malcolm Spier.

Nate Poulfry shifted his mass from his left ass cheek to his right and carefully considered his response. After several contemplative moments, he spoke.

"You need someone to bring this business back, to give it a voice, to revitalize it. You need someone who can perform with a modicum of craftsmanship, and I'm telling you, Malcolm, I can do it. The crowds are out there! They want to gather and listen and experience *real* music again, not this prepackaged auto-tuned disposable garbage. All I need from you – what I've always needed from you and this company – is money and exposure."

"Name Musiikki's top five downloads," Malcolm responded.

"Malcolm, what the fu…"

"Name them, Nate."

"You might as well ask me to name Craster's wives."

"Who the…? What the hell are you talking about, Nate? I'm sorry, but my answer is still no. Be sure to take care of yourself. You were and will always be one of my favorites."

Nate Poulfry's chin fell to his chest, taking with it his last remnants of hope. He stood, shook Malcolm's hand, and left the office at a quarter to noon.

Malcolm had never intended to degrade the

troubadour, but Nate Poulfry, the once revered folk-rock singer, was an anachronism. Unfortunately, the meeting had turned in the direction that Malcolm had hoped to avoid; it hadn't exactly been ugly, but it could not have been considered professional. Before Poulfry had shut the door, Malcolm began to regret his tone and his choice of words. At the height of his popularity, Poulfry had helped build Spier Records, but loyalty in this business could only be measured and tallied by the number of tickets an artist was able to sell. This was an unfortunate, callous statement that Malcolm had to make to a growing number of his 'dying' stars – and he detested it. Many were old friends, iconic musicians, voices of their generations, and Malcolm was forced to make them face the terrible immutable truth: their careers (lives) were over.

Fifty years before this embarrassing, degrading meeting, Malcolm's father had tirelessly negotiated to sign Nate and his band, The Poulfries. To do this, David Spier, with his teenage son in tow, had followed Poulfry and his band through the gloriously manic world of New York's sixties music scene. They had watched unforgettable shows at iconic venues like The Café au Go Go and The Electric Circus; they'd experienced their first wafts of weed and witnessed the outlandish effects that psychedelics had on young, beautiful people; they'd shared their first father-son beer – a piss-warm Rheingold – and Malcolm, working sans dad, had nervously caressed a just-legal pair of pert B cups. Through all the days and nights of the decade's musical haze, Poulfry had proved himself to be one of the greatest performers in the country, and after finally agreeing to sign with Spier Records, his fame and his fans had helped to build the budding record label into one of the industry's most innovative and profitable. Those resplendent days, however, were over, and that style of business was finished; the craft Malcolm had learned and honed was now buried under complex algorithms, fungible playlists, and infantile attention spans.

What little money Malcolm Spier had left could not be squandered on the relics and memories from his youth. He desperately needed those dwindling funds for cultivating young artists, yet he and his team had struggled for years to front run the trends and patterns of this new generation. The once trustworthy methods of discovering new talents and artists were as outdated as Nate Poulfry's unplugged sound. If Malcolm failed to find the solution soon, his father's business would wilt, wither, and die, and he would become what he dreaded most: forgotten.

While he had not inherited his father's affable nature, monetary connections, or radiant smile, Malcolm did have some valuable characteristics of his own: a seemingly clairvoyant ability in judging people's characters, an athlete's tenacity, and an incredibly shrewd mind. For a man in his early sixties, he kept active. He never bought into health trends, and what he couldn't work off, he hid under decent attire and a dark sense of humor. He was quite bald and quite thankful it was still in style. He loved his wife of thirty-three years, and as best as he could tell, she loved him, but their once animal attraction had faded into a tenuous companionship. She resented the hours he spent chasing phantom talents and dead-end trends, and he made little effort to make her feel needed, let alone loved. Their marriage and his business, if graphed side-by-side, were falling in perfect synchronicity. In the last fifteen years he hadn't been able to feel the pulse of the fans or his wife, and if he couldn't cultivate new prospects by the end of the quarter, Spier Records would join the ballooning list of dead music labels.

Deciding to leave early for lunch that afternoon turned out to be one of the few good ideas he'd had in weeks. As he strolled out of the lobby, he let his mind forget Nate Poulfry's depressing exit. He took his jacket off to let his body absorb the spring and turned his face to the sky to let his pale face roast. As he brought his eyes down to level, he finally noticed the season's influence on his city. The blooming Callery pears and freshly planted perennials painted the dreary façades in luminous azures, yellows, pinks, and whites. He walked up Eighth Street with a bounce in his step and decided to stop in his favorite café for an iced coffee.

The young couple's conversation was innocent and insignificant. They were enjoying their frothed lattes when the notifications of Rita Symone's death buzzed from their phones. Asphyxiation of the autoerotic variety, according to *celebdirrt.com*. Apparently safe words are difficult to pronounce with a seriously restricted airway. Ms. Symone was one of the last industry-molded pop stars from the nineties, and her career was predictably short, drug-laced, sex-laden, and utterly forgettable. Both the girl and her boyfriend were trying to remember, as they turned their phones downward and closed their eyes for a friendly intellectual duel, the exact dates of Symone's best performances, top singles, and album titles, but without the aid of the screens, all they could conjure up was the title of her sex tape – *Quiet Cummer: Rita Symone's Sexumentary*. It had done more for her popularity than all of her record sales combined. Most of the couple's banter was just filling time on a boring date until the woman noticed the inflated price of Symone's greatest hits on Musiikki.

"A buck-eighty for *Come Faster I'm Tired!*" she exclaimed.

"Two bucks for *Hidden Talents?*" the man asked incredulously.

"Twenty-two for *Party at Ground Zero?*"

"Nobody's gonna pay that, anyway. Search any torrent and we'll have them in less than a minute. I think I might still have my copy of *Quiet Cummer* at my place if you're interested?"

Even at the height of her popularity, many of the discussions that had revolved around Rita Symone had been about two things: selling merchandise or killing time. The coffee-drinking couple's exchange would have been categorized in the latter had Malcolm Spier not been listening. It took shape quickly, his first epiphany. In thirty seconds – it might have been ten, he had no idea because he had never had such a rush of thoughts – the nucleus had its necessary electrons – the people he might need, the equipment and connections – and finally, about a minute later, it morphed from a single atom into a beautifully balanced molecule. This excitement, this burst of cognitive energy must be what the greats felt before they started writing, composing, painting, drawing, cooking, inventing, or coding.

People moved around him as he had stopped in the north bound stream of pedestrians, but they didn't seem to mind or notice him staring at the sky, grinning like a sixth grader at his first schoolyard up-skirt show. His left oxblood wingtip moved first as his focus switched from the sky to his phone. He searched down through his contacts for Nate Poulfry. The couple's collective sticker shock had spurred Malcolm's idea for a new business model and rekindled his passion for folk-rock.

The jubilant phone call was too late to catch Poulfry before his plane left for Colorado, but he promised Malcolm he would be back in New York by the end of the week. It was actually several weeks before Nate found himself back at Spier's. The office seemed to be in controlled chaos: furniture blocked rooms and hallways; the fumes of fresh paint attacked his nostrils; newly framed records, posters, and paintings hung throughout the office, and teems of new faces careened from one room to another. A Benny Hill skit came to his mind.

Nate politely reached out to one of the ping ponging suits who happily directed him to the boss's new office. Malcolm greeted Nate with almost the same handshake and admiring expression that David Spier had given back in '67. The chair Nate sank into for this meeting was significantly more comfortable than the last.

"You know we can't offer you much in the way of a signing bonus – shit, I can't even pay myself much these days – but what I can promise you is time with the best producers I know, local bookings at the most popular venues around – places like Beat Nic's, Unplugged, Leute Geists, and Packies – and a carefully coordinated campaign to promote your remastered classics."

Nate had never been incredibly emotional in front of others, but the possibilities and prospects for this future were too overwhelming. He began a weeping laughter, but tried to keep himself composed.

"I'm telling you, Malcolm," he said through tearing eyes, "this is going to be my second coming, and I've been ready for years. I'll need a little bit of time to get myself and the band warmed up, but we're ready. Malcolm… your father would be proud."

Malcolm shook Nate's hand and walked him toward the open office door.

"Let me introduce you to one of our newest talent scouts, Nate. This is Makayla Rogers, and she'll be overseeing every aspect of your amazing comeback."

II

Makayla was enamored with her new boss and the new scene. She had listened to and followed some pretentious assholes early in her career. As a desperate-to-please intern, she'd obediently followed mortgage schemes, imaginary coins, and, finally, some steaming pile of shit called cloud commodities. She felt jaded by the tender age of twenty-seven. The gateways that her education should have opened – those boundless pathways her counselors and teachers had promised would be opened by volunteering, tutoring, abandoning her friends for academics, and running on several hours of sleep a night – had led only to repeated disappointments and dead ends. She had sacrificed her social life through most of her undergrad and graduate years for school work and part-time employment. After she had earned both of her degrees, she discovered the oft overstated joy of the working world: every new opportunity she pursued and every new job posting she answered had hundreds of candidates who were just as smart, just as talented, and just as qualified as she was. Most others came with far stronger connections, too.

She was a Chicago native who defected to New York to pursue her MBA and gainful employment. She shared a tiny apartment with two roommates in a less than gentrified part of Brooklyn, and she had little in the way of choice of where to go and what to do. Over the summer, her mother had delivered Makayla's father to the dementia ward at Chicago's VA hospital. Although his dementia was still manageable, Mrs. Etta Rogers had had enough of caring for her once unfaithful perennially cantankerous husband. Before Jordan Rogers's first VA meal was cold, Etta was on a flight to Paris, the first of many cities she had dreamed of while stuck in a fraudulent marriage. She graciously bankrolled the excursion with the sale of their co-op. With only meager savings, Makayla had packed what she could fit into her father's Honda and made her way east.

After finishing her degree and finding nothing in the corporate milieu, she took the only job she could find: selling organic coffee at the shop down the street from Spier Records. Makayla's med school roommate had introduced her to the manager of Café Tierra, and three years later, she began every morning with her mantra:

"I've got an MBA, I'm hemorrhaging student loans, I'm selling coffee."

Om Mani Padme Hum.

Malcolm entered the café on one of the many beautiful April afternoons and placed his order with his favorite barista. They'd got to know each other superficially, the way a professor softens to his favorite students over the course of a semester. They exchanged their usual friendly flirtations, but this order ended a bit differently; as Makayla handed Malcolm his receipt, he scribbled an address, phone number, and date for her to interview at the new Spier Records and Entertainment. She accepted the note somewhat skeptically, but decided that this old man was no alpha predator. The only thing she really had to be afraid of, the only clear and present danger that would not allow her restful nights, was that her employment options were diminishing faster than her father's mind.

Her interview had lasted several hours, and she spent a large part of it filling out profile questionnaires.

When asked about her weaknesses, a question she never knew how to answer properly, she tried to explain that she had always had an eclectic taste in music and that she used to see as many shows as she could, but the business end of the entertainment industry was entirely foreign to her. Malcolm assured her that candidates who were already deeply intimate with the industry were not being considered. He told her that many of the people he had trained and worked with in the past were often looking to poach clients and go off independently. He was looking for, as he simply said, "The right loyal people." He also assured her, using his newfound confidence, that her physical attributes, proportionately perfect both north and south, complimented her mind beautifully. She wondered, if she got the job, whether they'd watch the sexual harassment training video together.

She was happy to discover in a succinct congratulatory letter that she'd been selected to join the company and that in her upcoming orientation she would be training to become a talent scout. As a talent scout, Makayla would have a very specific job; it was one (according to her questionnaire results) perfectly tailored to her personality. All she would have to do was follow Spier's two-step model and she would have all the success she was ever promised. Her first few weeks were filled with the typical glitches and snafus, but she learned quickly, brought many of the elder statesmen up to speed with social media, and earned Malcolm's admiration and trust.

The first step in a talent scout's approach, according to Malcolm's new method, was infantile in its simplicity: reach out to old, desperate agents and artists, and if that didn't prove to be viable, scour the tabloids for any talents who intimated at the slightest inkling of making a return. Nate's situation had been a gift, he explained, so they could not wait for the talent to come to them. Desperation was paramount. Initially this struck Makayla as a very odd route for generating profits for a music/entertainment label. Her first inclination, as one whose job it is to seek out the gifted, was to search for young, hungry artists who could begin and sustain a trend. This was not the direction Spier wanted to go in, however. After being assigned as Poulfry's talent scout, Makayla understood why.

The second step was professional seduction.

"Again, you're dealing with the desperate," he assured her. "Feeding an addict what it needs should not be difficult, and these users haven't had their fixes in years. Many claim to be sober, claim to have found peace, claim to be above the need for fame and notoriety. Spier Records and Entertainment knows bullshit when it's interviewed at a cast reunion, or appears in a documentary, or attempts to pen memoirs. These junkies are never beyond the once loving cameras and awards. Their old pushermen are dead, and we're an entirely new cartel."

Malcolm continued explaining step two.

"Reach out to them. Dine with them. Keep it professional – the parameters of professionalism are entirely left to our scouts, Makayla. Promote the musicians at small venues at first, get them back into the scene. Be honest with them, and help them develop their revised images. As their reputations grow, we'll crank the nostalgia machine into action. In time you will blend their new image with their old one by promoting anniversary editions and album reissues. The artists will be hooked – how could they possibly resist?"

The key to the entire strategy was to sign the talent as cheaply as possible – not insultingly so, just below market value – and then get them to agree to transfer all rights and royalties for their old materials to their new representatives. The finesse of this exchange would have to be delicate; many of these musicians loved their early records as parents (good ones, at least) love their children. Some, though, were happy to be rid of the past; they were ready for the transformation. Malcolm and his team knew that this process had to be done by the right type of person: a person like the one Malcolm had chosen from his favorite coffee shop.

There were many scouts in addition to Makayla, and all types of forgotten names sifted through the office. Her focus would be the musicians, but she learned that SR&E would start perusing forgotten actors, authors, radio personalities, athletes, and comedians as potential clients. Malcolm dreamed that his prospects would react just as Poulfry had; he hoped they would all fall in love as they had in their formative years. He hoped that they would happily fire old agents and put everything with Malcolm and his team. He hoped that they would sign over all they had in order to live as their glorious former selves.

III

At the official signing ceremony, Nate didn't recognize the new receptionist, talent coordinators, or producers at the refurbished offices of SR&E (new sign, too?), but each employee greeted him with an enthusiastic smile and handshake. He didn't mind whose hand he pumped after he had met with Malcolm and Makayla. The exact numbers of his deal didn't concern Nate – they never really had. The initial payment wasn't much, and Nate knew better than most how crippled the industry was. The offer would be oceans away from what he used to command, probably a pittance, but the bookings, venues, and promotions that Makayla had set up were perfect, filled with a new generation of causeless hippies. Poulfry hadn't been this soberly excited in decades. After the train of gleaming teeth, Malcolm finally greeted Nate with a bear hug and a bottle of sparkling wine.

"Welcome back, Nate! Let's hear it for him, people!"

The small group cheered and applauded the soon-to-be resurrected star. His classics began playing through the speakers, the corks popped like exploding plastic bags, and work halted for the afternoon. Nate made a paltry attempt to resist the drink, but this was just too much for him. He could control one drink after twelve years. For this chance, he had to. His mind unfolded only the best outcomes: he would be the voice of a new generation; he would bring truth and passion and love through his guitar; he would see the changes of the new world before he died. He finished his first glass of sparkling chardonnay and unlocked his acoustic case. Malcolm wanted the guitar signed? That is fine, he thought. That is absolutely fine. Being desired, being celebrated like this was the superficial part of the business he had always resisted, always deplored, but this scene exposed a part of him that hadn't been nurtured since he had been the icon of the sixties counterculture.

Nate brought another drink to his mouth and sent the stem skywards. He put the empty glass on the edge of a desk, strummed the six string, and began singing with rusty confidence.

> *"To those who know the tireless path,*
> *Its winds and wans and fruitless wrath,*
> *Childhood dreams of hope and love,*
> *It sheds them all…"*

Someone cut off Nate's crutch, and without the recording he mumbled through some of the old lyrics, but was buoyed by this staff who knew every word. As the lyrics came back to him, his voice grew sturdier, and he caught the gaze of the gorgeous woman who would nurture him back to glory and smiled at her. He and the new members of Spier's team sang along as if sat around a roaring bonfire. Colleagues, most only acquainted for days, or weeks at the most, sang into each other's faces, peaking at the choruses, terribly missing the higher notes, laughing at their drunken attempts, and all the while forging a bond of an idealistic group – a team who would revitalize an industry and save their beloved musicians. Nate barely paused between songs, the crowd refused to let ice-cubes jingle in empty glasses before refilling them, and Malcolm could hardly contain his laughter. Ties were loosened, blouses shed their buttons, and zippers stopped defying gravity. The glorious revival went deep into the night.

Booking shows, negotiating with vendors, and traveling with Poulfry and his new Poulfries was exhilarating for Makayla. After hours of dealing with club owners, overseeing studio sessions, setting up hotel reservations, and exhausting trips with the band, Makayla began to care for Nate like she had tried to do for her ailing father. She fired three nurses (ones selected from Malcolm's preferred list) before settling with one who could best mitigate Nate's arthritis, fatigue, and mood swings. The other nurses were all quite competent and each came with stellar credentials, but they also came with far too many scruples. None had been willing to tolerate his asinine questions, his subtle yet harassing fondling, or his demands for very personal post-show massages. Nate couldn't care less which nurse tended to him, but for Makayla it was becoming an incredibly irritating situation. She had so many tasks to coordinate that part of her just wanted the ladies – he would allow no male nurses – to tolerate Nate's behavior and fulfill his lewd requests. Her conscience as a woman railed against these thoughts – one of her proudest moments before quitting her last internship had been sending her supervisor to his knees after he'd suggested she go to hers – but her pragmatic-manager conscience wanted certain problems to work out without her interventions. All of the nurses had been aggravations until Malcolm personally recommended Alexis. Alexis Drison had been a homecare nurse, tasked with educating Malcolm's wife on managing her Type 2 diabetes, and when that job ended she found herself as a full-time employee in the offices of SR&E.

Alexis was professional and erudite in every part of her job. Her bedside manner was empathetic, and she immediately melded with Nate – Poulfry would not tolerate patronizing, demeaning health directives from a 'company-fucking nurse'. In their first few conversations, Alexis made it clear to Nate what he needed to do to maintain his health while on tour by presenting clear facts and recommendations in a succinct care plan. She never once tried to coerce or threaten him – she spoke to him like the intelligent, experienced adult he was – and he later told Makayla that they would all make a cozy trio.

The late-night shows in the city gradually morphed into small summer festivals up state, and for the fall, Makayla booked The Poulfries in Nate's hometown, Cristol Springs, Colorado, for Halloween and the famed Coffin Race. The pure satisfaction of her new job and life outweighed the constant travel, endless emailing, and Nate's annoying idiosyncrasies and demands. In spite of the chaos, she actually grew close him, and caught herself singing along not only to his classics, but to his new songs, too. Makayla began to realize the incredible depth to Nate's talent. He was as good a poet as he was a musician. He effortlessly articulated his frustrations, loves, hopes, hates, and beliefs with inventive imagery, impeccable rhythm, and captivating tones. Like his fans from decades past, she found herself mesmerized when he sang of lost innocence, unrequited love, and acts of condomless sex.

As the frequency of the shows increased, Makayla found that late bookings crippled the old man for days, so all upcoming after-hour venues were tentatively scrapped. After one very grueling show at Leute Geists, Nate, sprawled on his hotel bed, made a truly odd admission: he confessed to Makayla that while he loved his old fans, he didn't really want to see their drooping faces in the front rows. He said it was like looking into a grotesque panoramic mirror. He found it depressing as hell. From that point on he wanted to be surrounded by the youth he dreamed of inspiring, so Makayla began a massive social media campaign to spread the word. Though it started a rather vicious exchange, she convinced him that playing the late shows was the best way to attract fresh bodies to his audiences. He acquiesced, and Makayla instructed Alexis to begin a moderate supply of stimulants and painkillers to help him through it. He tried to object at first, tried to explain how sobriety had been the succor that saved his life.

"Alexis, the Lord and the Springs helped me out of that darkness, and I won't go back. I know I look like I have a virgin's stamina, but I'll get myself back into shape without that shit. No, I'm serious. I don't want it, and it won't be around here when I get back."

His objections grew quieter and less frequent, and finally disappeared when he saw his audiences filling up with young, ardent fans who chanted his name, sang his songs, and paid top dollar for all of his tickets.

IV

"How can you be here now, Mel?" asked Charlie Orin. He was Malcolm's oldest friend, trusted lawyer, and, as his accountant, a contortionist with numbers. "You should be out there trying to find out where the fuck she went!"

"And what the hell would I say to her if I found her, Charlie? She nearly burned the house down when she torched my memorabilia room. She took the dog, left the cat, and emptied its litter box onto our bed. You know what it felt like watching this shit on my surveillance recordings?"

"She needs help, Mel. She has for years."

"I can't help her. I've never been able to help her, and it's not like I didn't try. We got her plenty of antidepressants and she knows that she's got to lose weight for her diabetes, but she never keeps up with any of it. I had two options: save my wife or save my business, and I chose the one with better odds."

"I hope you made the right choice, my friend. Poulfry's numbers have been great, but it may not be enough. Your idea is innovative, but it is very costly to promote. I'll leave you alone, and if you want to go after her, or if you need anything, I'll be in my office."

The door had barely latched before Malcolm's phone rang. He let it ring five times before picking up.

"He's fucking dead, Malcolm!"

"Who is thi...Makayla? Who's dead? What the hell happened? Oh, fuck. I'll be on the next plane out. I want you to hang up the phone and call Charlie Orin – yes,

Orin. Tell him exactly what happened, and try to find your composure."

Malcolm was at JFK and on the 10:30am to Colorado Springs. It was a flight he would not do sober.

The tour was supposed to climax in Nate's hometown, Cristol Springs, Colorado. Picturesque was an understatement. Its mountainous beauty and tie-dyed culture had supported Nate Poulfry and his fans for decades. Nate had returned to it after years of alcohol and drug abuse, and along with professional help, the Springs' tranquility and purity had revitalized him. He had been elated to be playing for his hometown because now he could watch his fellow Coloradans career down Taskins Ave. (the base of Taskins Peak) in their macabrely decorated coffins. Teams and individuals spent months preparing for the Coffin Race, painting, testing, and hyping their adult pinewood racers, and the entire town came to watch and cheer. While the preparations were extensive, and showmanship encouraged, each coffin had to express a sense of personalization and talentless artistry. The race and its participants reflected the community and its oddities, and Nate had made a point never to miss it.

Poulfry and his entourage had flown directly from New York to Colorado while Makayla took a brief respite to visit her father in Chicago. She found him in decent physical condition, actually a bit heavier, but his mind seemed to be in quick decline. Several times he called her Etta and reached out for her more as a husband than as a father, but she calmly corrected him, moved him back to his bed, and tried to redirect him to their conversation. She told him all about her new job, and when he heard the name Nate Poulfry, he rattled off a story about the first concert he ever saw. The headliner had been Piny Jones and his special guests had been Pearle Collier and

The Oysters. He accurately (Makayla had heard this story many times before) recounted the venue, the year, and the name of the girl he fucked afterwards (well, that bit was new) in a thirty-second story. When Makayla asked if he'd want to talk with a famous musician, he just stared at her.

"Makayla, sweetheart? Aren't you going to be late to piano lessons?"

At this, she gave him his new fashionable Musiikki digital player (The MÜS), a pair of ear buds, and pressed play to start track one of Pearle Collier's first album, *My Baby's Ride.* When the title track began to play, her father mouthed the words, slowly at first, a second or so behind the great R&B singer, but ever so gradually he synched with his favorite song, and by the chorus he could have been on stage himself. The music echoed through the sealed crevices of his memories and brought two minutes and thirty seconds of clarity to his otherwise entropic mind.

When she rejoined the tour, her first call was to Alexis. Ten minutes after that conversation, Alexis knocked on Makayla's door and gave her the briefing on Nate's health, mood, and drug consumption. The locale had put him in an exultant mood, but his tan and stubbled face hid his rapidly degrading health. His blood pressure was now consistently one seventy over one hundred, and he was accepting increasingly larger quantities of painkillers. The late nights were beginning to wear on him the most and Alexis did her best to rejuvenate him after each show, but he was fading as fast as his fame was growing. This was everything Makayla didn't want to hear. She made a few notes to add to her profile, thanked Alexis, and went to bed.

Every part of the final Halloween show had been ethereal. The musician and audience, including Makayla and Alexis, were harmoniously enamored and perfectly sublime. Makayla couldn't believe that she had, at the last possible minute, arranged to have it recorded. She was still concerned with Nate's health, but her suggestion that he return directly to the hotel after the show were met with an indignant response about her knowing her speed and staying in her fucking lane. She watched from stage right and accepted the fact that the old man knew his boundaries. This was Nate's night after all, and he seemed to be conjuring every part of his lost youth and energy to entertain this sold out crowd. She was as pleased with herself as she was with him. As she watched, she felt a light brush against her hand and turned to find Alexis's beautifully captivating eyes.

Makayla awoke with the daze and confusion of a restless night. She slid a leg off the bed and felt the cool air attack her naked body. She rubbed her eyes with her right thumb and index finger, and turned her head to see Alexis sleeping on her side, the sheet tucked under her left arm. She smiled as she headed for the shower. Her tip-toed sprint to the bathroom was cut off by a violent succession of knocks on her room door. She quickly found a robe and a pair of slippers and asked who it was.

"Ms. Rogers?" the voice asked frantically.

"Yes. Who are you?"

"Ms. Rogers, please open the door. I'm Andrew Colby, the hotel manager. We spoke and met yesterday morning. Please, Ms. Rogers, this is very urgent."

Alexis had awoken with the thunderous knocking and had made her way into the bathroom. Makayla tied her robe and opened the door to find an extremely pale, nervous hotel manager.

"Ms. Rogers, OK, Makayla, I'm afraid you have to come with me to Mr. Poulfry's room immediately. The ambulances are on their way."

Ambulance was not the word she wanted to hear. She ran past Andrew Colby and up two flights of stairs to Nate's suite. She cursed herself for not waiting; of course the door wouldn't be wide open, but seconds later the manager caught up with his skeleton card in hand. They entered the room as the housekeeper had found it: Nate's body lay on the floor in a concoction of his own fluids. Vomit and piss mixed horrifically with excrement, a small bottle of pills, and a spilled bottle of locally distilled whiskey.

"Oh, fuck," she whispered. "Oh, Nate."

She started to move toward the prostrate body, but was stopped by Colby's voice.

"Ms. Rogers, please, I wouldn't touch anything until the police arrive," he said in a tone mixed with anxiety and horror.

She froze at his words. Shortly after, the medics arrived and instructed both of them to clear a path. Although they moved quickly to the old man, it became apparent that resuscitation was not an option. They didn't begin CPR. This body would now be the property of the county coroner. Makayla absently told Colby that she needed to get back to her room for her clothes and for her phone. She drifted down the hall like a phantom meandering to a haunt.

"Ms. Rogers," said a police officer standing just outside of the room, "please don't leave the hotel until we've had a chance to speak with you."

She nodded and went back downstairs to find Alexis dressed and waiting by the door.

"What the hell is going on, Makayla? What's wrong?"

Makayla regained some use of her brain and ran past Alexis, going directly for the phone. When she heard Makayla's conversation with Malcolm, Alexis threw the door open and sprinted to Nate's suite.

*

Malcolm arrived incredibly disheveled, but he was determined to make sure that his employees (those still alive) were properly cared for, and more importantly, not doing or saying anything that might harm the label. He rented a car and set out on the two hour trip to Cristol. He arrived to find the hotel blocked by a mass of hung-over wailing fans. He followed an officer's instructions to detour down the block, parked, and while walking back toward the hotel, heard the fans' cries of despair and shock. Before he got absorbed into the mourning audience, he made a call to the hotel's front desk and asked for the manager. In a couple of minutes, a tall, gaunt man exited the lobby's spinning door and acknowledged Malcolm's waving hand. They shook hands and entered through a side entrance, circumventing the masses.

He met Makayla and Alexis down the hall from Nate's suite. Both were visibly perturbed, but were able to lead the way to suite 217.

"That's fucking creepy," Malcolm said in a whisper. He didn't bother to explain the coincidence to his distraught employees. Makayla and Alexis spoke quietly with the uniformed officer at the door, and after doing a quick search for the detectives and medical examiner, she let Malcolm view the morbid scene from the doorway. He felt like he was looking at a staged section in a haunted house. Part of him expected, and the other part hoped, that Nate's corpse would quickly turn its head for the climactic scare, but the putrid smell destroyed the fantasy. No, the body wouldn't move. Malcolm's mind wandered back to the last trip he ever took with his father. David Spier had enjoyed Malcolm's Vegas bachelor party more than many of the younger cohorts. He had been able to handle the drugs – he'd done copious amounts of them through the seventies – but the hooker's intensity had proved too much for him. He had died in peak-thrust, and the panicked entrepreneur had writhed free, taken her cash, and split. She had left him face down in a pillow, spurting ejaculate in either the greatest or worst demise ever experienced. This, Malcolm lamented, was the memory conjured by Nate's foul lifeless body.

"Excuse me! What the hell are you doing up here? This is a crime scene not a peep show!"

Detective Ray Delijo was in no mood to deal with any more diehard fans. His bellowing question ripped Malcolm from his memories and focused him to the present.

"I'm sorry, Detective…"

"Delijo."

"I'm Malcolm Spier, Nate's manager, and I just needed to see him for myself. We'll leave immediately. Again, I'm sorry. Please, we didn't mean to interfere with anything."

Delijo calmed his tone and said, "Mr. Spier, just try to understand that until we've ruled out any foul play, we're considering this an active crime scene. Officer Arnold, please escort them downstairs."

V

Settling the affairs in Colorado took several weeks. Malcolm and Makayla worked tirelessly to contact Nate's two remaining relatives (an estranged son and a sister), and then to provide the authorities with any information they could. When that was finished, they paid off the remaining crew members and moved them to other assignments, and, finally, they oversaw the breakdown of the massive stage. Back in his office, Malcolm lamented what he saw as having been his last chance; even before Nate had played a note, Malcolm and Charlie had roundly figured Poulfry's value. It had been very promising, but Malcolm had banked on Poulfry's success attracting, as it had in the past, other former stars to reach for that brass one final time. Now, though, he had passing thoughts of screwing his creditors by taking a header off SR&E's roof. After rolling some rough figures and ideas in his mind, he realized that the business his father had started would be gone by the spring. He folded his arms onto his desk and laid down his head to weep. When he had finally worked up some tears, Charlie knocked on his door and let himself in.

"Mel, pick your head up and listen to this."

Malcolm slowly picked his head up to humor his old friend.

"Malcolm, I'm serious. Listen to what I'm going to tell you. Nate Poulfry's singles, albums, videos, books, and merchandise are selling for three-to-five times the amount they were worth before he OD'd. Malcolm, film studios have been calling asking about buying the rights to documentaries and biopics, copies of his final show have completely sold out, been uploaded, and gone viral, and tributes are sprouting up all over the world. This is going to be fucking huge, Mel, and we own the rights to all of it."

Malcolm turned to the signed guitar mounted on his wall. He replayed the information in his mind as he dried his eyes with the cuffs of his sleeves, then stood from his chair and ran to give Charlie an 'our-team-just-scored-the-winning-fucking-touchdown' bear hug. Charlie, two feet off the ground, let out a victorious holler and threw his papers to the ceiling. Malcolm's mind whirled and he dropped Charlie back to the ground.

"I can't believe the bastard is worth more in the ground than he was out on the road. Charlie, where's the closest Poulfry vigil?"

Charlie adjusted his jacket and responded, "Up in the Park, I think. You want to run up there?"

"Let me clean up a bit. Grab Makayla and meet me in front of Café Tierra in ten."

Malcolm changed out of his sweat-stained shirt and slacks to a light sweater and jeans. He turned on his TV to see if Charlie was right; his friend was not one for hyperbole, but some things need to be realized with your own eyes. Charlie wasn't exaggerating in any way. Poulfry was all over the music channels, the twenty-four hour news channels, and entertainment news shows. He killed the TV, threw on his coat, and took the stairs to the lobby.

Makayla couldn't figure out Charlie's vibrant mood; he looked like he was selling a revolutionary detergent on an infomercial. She, on the other hand, had been content to sulk in her office, getting reacquainted, comfortable even, with her familiar feelings of failure and regret.

Since they'd arrived back in New York, she had actually been waiting for Malcolm or Charlie to come in and fire her – having your first client die in his hometown doesn't normally foster promotions or accolades. Charlie, however, spoke no words of the termination when he poked his head through her open door.

"Grab your coat, and let's go see a vigil," he said.

He didn't give her the chance to consider the options. In three steps he had her coat over his forearm, and in two more he was next to her desk with a smile on his face. That damn smile was infectious, and she did feel like a walk in the crisp fall could do nothing but help.

The trio left the café with black coffees and briskly walked toward the subway. They joked and laughed as Charlie caught up on the office gossip. Malcolm was able to affirm his suspicions about Makayla's fling with Alexis, an experience she confirmed as being much more than a fling. This news piqued Charlie's interest, but Makayla coyly changed the subject and pointed out their upcoming stop. Charlie didn't object; he told her that his imagination would more than fill in the details.

As they got closer to the park, the chatter decreased, quieted, stopped. It wasn't out of rudeness or boredom: each was awestruck by the crowd mourning the death of Nate Poulfry. Makayla, a product of the artist-from-a-talent-show generation, couldn't believe that any musician could have this type of influence on his fans. Charlie couldn't believe that this many people didn't have something else to do. Malcolm couldn't believe how many young fans rallied, sang, and mourned for a man old enough to be their grandfather. He saw not only respect, but possibilities. If this many people, both old and young, were still paying their respects, they were also still paying for merchandise. This was a market he had never considered. This amazing spectacle sparked his next epiphany.

They spent two hours singing, swaying, and emoting with the Park Poulfrites. For Malcolm and Makayla, it was the catharsis they had had to deny themselves in Colorado. Makayla suggested some food, and Malcolm added a suggestion of drinks, and Charlie suggested a great place on Second and Seventy-sixth.

The three of them found a quiet booth in a dimly lit section at the back of the bar. They drank seasonal ales and ordered their burgers medium-well. What little conversation occurred amid the chewing was conspicuously one-sided. Malcolm, draining half his beer, began a prophetic speech, speaking as much to himself as he was to his old and new friend.

"Being a part of that service in the Park – that's honestly what it was – reminded me of a lesson from my favorite King novel: nostalgia fucking sells. While I don't have the supernatural talents of his characters, I do have the mind to understand that death, in the right circumstances, can be very lucrative. Now, what Nate Poulfry showed me," he paused as the waitress delivered another round, "is that death doesn't have to be unpredictable and mysterious. If I, we, Spier Records and Entertainment, could own and control the comeback storyline of the public's most revered artists, we can make a fortune. Now bringing back an old singer/songwriter will make us a few bucks, as long as every part of the revival goes smoothly, but if we could also control the narratives of their deaths, as the elderly and infirm are apt to experience, we would be able to make a whole lot more. But why should we have to wait for these ailments, addictions, accidents, or incidents of age? Makayla? Charlie?"

He looked from one to the other, and they gazed back with blank cultish stares.

"What we need to do is add one more step to the SR&E method – a step three: *we* kill the talent."

He said nothing more, took a chunk out of his burger, and stared at them over the seedless bun. For the briefest of instants, Makayla saw something that terrified her, something primal and predatory in his chewing. He patiently waited for their reactions. The ones he got didn't surprise him. Charlie smiled, reached for his burger, and ate as if listening to an old kook waxing poetic about the glory days. Makayla sat frozen, not because she believed her boss was serious, but because what he said actually made sense. She remained still for an instant longer to chastise those thoughts and to quickly contemplate her life to this point. She thought of her father, the demented old vet living in that VA shithole; she thought of her failed jobs and hollow relationships; she thought of her options if she left SR&E. Malcolm, while looking like he would be a perfect roommate for her father, had given her a genuine taste of success. His third step, while frightening, seemed terrifyingly sound. These people were near their ends anyway, right? Some leech would always be looking to capitalize on the tragedies of others, so why shouldn't those leeches be her and her team? After a couple of minutes of contemplating these thoughts, she went to the bathroom, emptied her bladder, regained her composure, and made her way back to the booth. She ordered a stronger drink, waited until it came, and spoke pensively. Both Charlie and Malcolm listened.

"How would we do this, Malcolm? How would we do this without going to jail for the rest of our lives?"

Malcolm joined her with another round, drank another large gulp, and smiled

"So there are no objections to the new step? Excellent. We'll discuss what I've come up with back at the office."

Part Two

Refurbishing Pearle Collier and Seeing the Seitz

VI

At about the same time Makayla Rogers was pleading with Nate Poulfry to venture back to late-night performances, Malcolm was sitting in his office, contemplating whether or not he should answer a call from his old acquaintance, Sylvan Thoreau. He had left a message for the sweet old bastard the day before, but was beginning to second guess his choice. He didn't know if Sylvan still had any ties with his ex-wife and former client, Pearle Collier. He didn't know if the visceral, emotional gospel she sang in her awe-inspiring four-octave voice would strike the same passions as it had back in the early sixties. He was confident in Poulfry's increasing popularity, and the company should be diversifying its portfolio, but he was dubious about the popularity of R&B. He did, though, need another immediate talent in his arsenal, so he decided to pick up the receiver.

"Malcolm, Malcolm Spier! How the hell are you? You've made it this long and you don't have a chesty blond answering your calls? Shit, how are you? It's been what, twenty...twenty-three years?"

"Thoreau, you old schmuck, will you let me at least get a hello in?" Malcolm said with a laugh.

"There, you said it. It's great – you feel better about yourself, now? What the hell have you been up to, and why the hell am I reading about Nate Poulfry again? You seriously rolled that old hippie out of his Indian prayer mat to play music in public? Shit, you could probably squeeze the resin out of his clothes and sell it in Colorado.

My God, man, it is good to talk with you again."

"What the hell have you been up to? You seem to know every damn move in my life, so I might as well listen to your ridiculous trials and tribulations."

"Damn, Spier, where to start. I've been scraping by on social security checks and living the high life off of shitty dividends. I must be the last prick in this country who still gets damn dividend checks. Malcolm, most of my clients split for retirement or split for their permanent retirements years ago. My kids swing down with the grandkids every February to piss in my pool and litter on the beach, and I spend my days drinking, sleeping, and gardening. That's really about it. What the hell can I do for you, my friend?"

"Syl, I need to know if you're still in any type of contact with Pearle."

Malcolm didn't like Sylvan's immediate and obvious silence. To this point, the conversation had been conducted lopsidedly, as if Sylvan were a dentist speaking to a patient whose mouth was filled with gauze, tubes, and instruments, helplessly unable to respond, yet now the loquacious old man was muted.

"Shit, Mel," Sylvan was the only person other than Charlie who called him this, "I haven't heard from her in over a decade. Last I knew she was trying to produce her nephew's career, but I don't recall hearing the albums. The last time I saw her was when everyone else did – you remember it? Two years ago at her first producer's tribute show. She still sounded incredible, but I haven't seen her in person or spoken with her since we finalized the divorce. I mean, there have been a few Christmas cards, but nothing that's actually meaningful…What has you interested with her anyway? You're not thinking about sending her out with Nate Poulfry, are you?"

"No, nothing like that, Syl, but you wouldn't believe

how fast Nate's tour is taking off. I'm not shitting you. He's been selling out clubs across the city. I wish we'd had social media – social media, Syl, the phones and the Internet – when we were starting out. His name and tracks and merch have been exploding. I figured if we had one more name with Poulfry's recognition, one more nostalgia machine, we could really become something huge. Of course, Syl, if you can get her back into my studios, I'd bring you in completely."

"Mel, I…I don't know…I…"

"You wouldn't have to travel or tour or leave the damn city, Syl. All you'd have to do is coordinate and negotiate like you used to. I've got a hell of a great team now. They're young, hungry, and constantly seeking praise. They'll look up to you, buddy. They'll actually listen to your bullshit stories and laugh at your awful jokes, and you won't have to wait for quarterly dividend checks."

"All I can say is that I'll try, Mel. It was damn good talking with you. Get yourself a fucking secretary, will ya?"

Malcolm hung up the phone and laughed. He knew that the old man was sitting in his house, rehearsing what he'd say to his ex-wife: the voluptuous, the supremely talented, Pearle Collier.

VII

Thoreau was doing exactly what Malcolm thought he was, except as he rehearsed his opening lines, he tore his office apart looking for Collier's number. When he finally found her entry in his address book, he began to sweat. It wasn't fear really, though that was part of it, but an anxious excitement usually reserved for a last-round interview or an actor's opening night. Their affair had blossomed out of the romantic tradition of proximity. They'd kept it relatively quiet and clandestine in the beginning; those days were still unforgiving to the union of his whiteness and her blackness, but as the years passed, her voice and his connections catapulted her to stardom and to the top of every pop chart in the country. Gradually they began to ignore society's norms and opinions. In the spring of 1970, they had married in a lavish ceremony on the streets of New Orleans. There were parades, brass bands, drinks, speeches, dancing, and the endless possibilities of two beautifully talented lovers. Pearle, unpretentiously, was the center of the festivities. She sang only one song with her Oysters, but when she did, Bourbon Street turned its collective ear. She was quite petite, the singular characteristic that confounded most producers, beautiful with chestnut eyes and charcoal black hair that she wore naturally, and as quick witted as any late-show host. Sylvan knew how lucky he was, but she also counted herself as blessed; she would not have settled for anyone who was simply trying to ride her talent to the Promised Land.

As the seventies progressed into the eighties, trends

in music changed. The couple's identities morphed, and a physical and emotional schism grew between them. They became different people. She split with her group, produced a moderately successful solo career, and experienced the world as an independent woman. He worked with a greater focus on younger talents and new genres, but managed to keep up with his estranged wife through letters and phone calls. They were separating amicably enough; neither was causing direct stress to the other or making any sincere attempts to salvage the relationship. The lawyers at the divorce described the exchange like a chaperoned first date. Both Pearle and Sylvan joked, exchanged anecdotes, and remarked on their progressing ages, changed styles, and dyed hair. Both attorneys swore that they had witnessed nastier exchanges at house closings.

Now, though, Sylvan sat with her number in front of his reading glasses. He picked up the house phone and dialed. After an abnormal five rings, someone picked up the receiver.

"Collier residence. To whom do I owe the pleasure?" asked a delicate voice.

"Pearle…it's Sylvan…Sylvan Thoreau."

"Syl! My goodness, how are you? How many years has it been? Ten? Twelve?

"Honestly, darling, when I just heard your voice, it felt like only hours."

"Goodness gracious with the *darling*, Sylvan. If it's going to be that kind of call, let me draw the curtains and light some candles."

Her laughter brought a smile to his face and a warmth to his heart that had been missing for over thirty years.

"So what do I owe this surprise?" she asked.

"Pearle, I will tell you eventually, but please let me hear that laugh again."

"Say something amusing."

"I was the best lay you ever had."

"I said something amusing, my dear, not something true."

At this response, he was legitimately concerned for his heart. He felt it tighten like a hamstring just before the snap. He took a deep breath, steadied his voice, and continued.

"Pearle, to borrow a line from the immortal *Blues Brothers*, I'm thinking of getting the band back together."

Malcolm was leaving one of Poulfry's evening gigs, a very successful session at Beat Nic's, when he got Sylvan's call. The news that came through his phone's earpiece fitted perfectly with the plans he had already put in motion. In between helping Makayla navigate the industry and managing a new team, he had been haunting local jazz and R&B clubs for availabilities and prices. He wouldn't give the promoters the name of his talent, and in return they were pretty vague about what they would pay and offer, but he was confidently able to estimate that when Pearle Collier was ready to sing, there would be somewhere for her to do it. He then blocked out time in his studio and reserved (for an outrageous sum) Andres Marr, one of the industry's premiere R&B producers, but he didn't regret the cost. He knew the old adage: to make it, you have to spend it. Malcolm also knew that convincing Pearle to get back into a tour would be a monumental challenge, but getting her back on stage with The Oysters would be nearly impossible. While Poulfry's situation had been a gift to SR&E (the bearded old codger had come to him like a beggar after all), Malcolm's tone and finesse would have to be altered entirely to court Collier. His gamble with Thoreau had paid off, and now he had to set his team out to find – if there were any left – the remaining women of Pearle's backup group, The Oysters. He made a mental note never to call them *the backups* in their presences. There had been at least three iterations of singers, but Malcolm didn't think they would be hard to locate. A few had tried to branch out on their own, but most had accepted their fifteen minutes and moved on to private lives. Malcolm would give the softball assignment to a small cadre of interns.

Two days later, Thoreau called with better news than Malcolm could have hoped for. Pearle Collier wanted to meet with Malcolm and the SR&E team. Sylvan explained to Malcolm that she had always respected the way in which the company had been run and maintained, and that she fondly remembered David Spier's honesty, integrity, and dedication to his artists. As an amateur and a professional, Pearle had always made it a point to know which companies had treated their talents like human beings and which companies had treated them like livestock.

Sylvan went on to say that he thought there might be an ulterior reason for Collier's willingness to perform, but he seemed either too embarrassed or too timid to explain what the hell it was. Malcolm had some trouble getting his old friend to voice the stipulation, but with a bit of flattery and some dashes of chicanery and patience, Sylvan finally divulged that Pearle was still trying to help develop her nephew's music career, and her terms went thusly: she would do a little singing and touring for Malcolm if SR&E would agree to sign her horn playing nephew, Everett Beechum, to the label. Malcolm couldn't believe that was all she wanted. This wasn't a negotiation – this was two for the price of one.

"Sylvan, if that's all she wants, we can have this going by next week. Let me run a few things by Charlie before I make promises I can't keep. I'll get back to you later on tonight. Yeah, sure, tomorrow's fine, too. Syl, you sly bastard, this is going to be huge."

After he hung up with Thoreau, Malcolm trotted down the hall and took the stairs to Charlie's office. They talked over the rough numbers, tried to anticipate any legal surprises, and finally decided on their counteroffer: SR&E would sign both, on the conditions that Collier sing one reunion show with The Oysters, sign all rights to her old material over, and that Beechum start out as a member of her band. Malcolm waited until after dinner to make the call. The relay between Sylvan and Pearle and Sylvan and Malcolm actually took several days, and Malcolm took his turn sweating. He wasn't used to information taking this long to travel, but his patience was rewarded.

Sylvan's call was a compilation of great news: Pearle Collier wanted to meet to sign the agreement by the end of the week; the companies that owned the legal rights to The Oysters' biggest hits had dissolved years ago, and her foremost co-writer, Marvin Diggs, had died in a car accident back in '97. She was the sole proprietor of her lyrics, music, and image. In addition to this incredible news, she also wanted Sylvan Thoreau by her side to go over every detail. Malcolm hung up his phone, turned on the office stereo, and let Pearle Collier's voice resonate throughout every speaker in the building. She sang in her seductively sensual tone:

> *"What you missed,*
> *It wasn't hard to find.*
> *What he touched in me*
> *It was right inside.*
> *What you lost, I don't pay no mind.*
> *'cause now I'm sittin' here smilin'*
> *Waitin' for my baby's ride."*

He hummed along and danced down to Charlie's office.

VIII

The still radiant Pearle Collier and the surprisingly debonair combination of Sylvan Thoreau and Everett Beechum harmonized perfectly with the casually refined Malcolm Spier and Charlie Orin. The elder parties shared stories of the good times gone by. They reminisced over the names that had brought so much joy and laughter, and then mourned the fact that those names were now more frequently celebrated in the obituaries than on the front pages – Everett didn't bother to point out that barely anyone read front pages anymore. The intimate third floor conference room was adorned with Gold records, rare Warhol's, and David Spier's collection of autographed pictures and portraits. Two pitchers of ice water and five glasses sat on top of the oval-shaped mahogany table, and Everett, having little to contribute to the nostalgia, found his way the keyboard in the corner of the room and began to tickle its keys. This signing felt more like a friendly card game than a business agreement; Malcolm made no secret of his admiration for Collier's talent and reputation, and she spoke and laughed with him and Charlie as if they were reunited college roommates. There was no need for coercion or threats or bullshit. After one particularly funny story, Pearle poured a glass of water and got down to her version of business.

"Malcolm...I like you, and Charlie...you seem sweet, too. Syl vouched for you both, and you've affirmed every one of his words. After so many years and so many pricks, I've come to trust my friends and first impressions.

Now I'm not looking to get rich again, and I took full advantage of my time in the light. I won't lie to you – not yet at least – being in front of those audiences again would feel special, but I want my legacy to live on through those who deserve it, and Everett is the one who does."

Everett's playing ceased as soon as his aunt began speaking, and when she concluded, he had taken his seat to her left. There was absolutely no arrogance in his demeanor, and his respect for his aunt was absolute. He had played quietly during their conversation, not out of the frustration of being ignored, but out of his love of the art. He was never far from any instrument – he could play almost any of them – and he thought the moment was opportune for composing. The four free spirits had barely noticed that he had set their life stories to theme music.

He had never tried to make his career off his aunt's name. His talent was natural and undeniable, yet he had been born into the wrong generation. His music, unlike the listening public, had depth and substance, and these qualities confused record companies that were desperate for quick-money acts and marketable gimmicks. The last thing they would consider was spending the time or money to produce and nurture musicians like him properly, so he got used to being a talented vagrant. Aunt Pearle helped all she could, but there were limits to her resources, and he wouldn't see his godmother left destitute in her autumnal years. He had reached his limits with the industry – their laziness and incompetence were infuriating. He had become frustrated with himself – he was no longer the child prodigy, and he was now considered to be far too old to sell to the demographics that counted. His demographics. His target listeners. More than anything else, he had become frustrated with his damn audiences. They avoided buying and listening to complete albums like they avoided reading stories over a hundred pages. For Everett, cherry-picking single tracks instead of absorbing the nuances and artistry of an entire album was the equivalent of an apathetic student reading Cliff's Notes simply to get through his assigned readings. You're not supposed to just *get through* art, he constantly told an audience of one. When Pearle called him with the news of this meeting he had been hanging around the Lower Ninth Ward (his roots) to play in clubs, weddings, and private parties. He had canceled his last job, packed his horn, and immediately made his way to Baton Rouge.

The trip to New York would be a grand finale for Pearle's career, and, for Everett, the comeback opportunity for a career that never was. He was happy that Pearle trusted these new faces; he'd been in this long enough to know the frauds from the...When he really thought about it, he couldn't think of a solitary one that he considered sincere or trustworthy. Malcolm and Charlie seemed different; not entirely free of that aura of corporate bullshit, but respectable. He trusted his instincts and was happy to have them confirmed by his aunt and her ex-husband, Sylvan. Malcolm Spier spoke candidly and succinctly about Everett's role on his aunt's tour, and the tone was consistently professional; they didn't make his stint as the backup player sound degrading. After fulfilling his obligations to Pearle, he would go to work and record with Andres Marr, and SR&E would lead him as close to the waters as they could.

"Glad you're pleased with the deal, Mr. Beechum," Malcolm said proudly.

So my poker face needs a bit of tweaking, Everett thought as he looked at the smiling executive.

"Anything I can do to help Aunt Pearle, Mr. Spier."

Charlie passed the contract to Pearle Collier, and she, Sylvan, and Everett studied it closely. Malcolm went to the cabinet, lifted out a carafe, and poured himself a stiffer drink than ice water. He didn't make any offers to share; he wanted their focus on the words. He drank alone, staring at the magnificent skyline. He drank until the ice jostled against the sides of the glass He returned to the table, and each party signed in black, shook hands, and agreed to a celebratory lunch.

IX

Makayla only became aware of the company's acquisition of Pearle Collier months later, after she had returned from Colorado and listened to Malcolm's post-Poulfry epiphany. Hearing the news about Collier hadn't really stirred her sense of excitement or hope; the famous name registered somewhere in her brain, but she was still in shock from Nate's death, and, as she perceived it, her utter failure. When she had returned from Cristol Springs, she had spent the first few days back in the office playing single-player hide n' seek: when she had to leave her office, she darted with her head down and avoided human contact as best she could. Her appetite seemed to have died with Poulfry, so lunches out with colleagues wouldn't be an issue. She saw unemployment as a looming phantom waiting at the end of every dimly lit hallway and stairwell, ready to pounce and drag her back to her pitiful barista duties. She came in relatively late in the mornings and left noticeably early in the afternoons, but neither Malcolm nor Charlie raised any objections. Both of them were fairly foreign to emotions, especially those emitted by others, so they gave her space to cope. Makayla didn't need a shoulder to cry on, but she thought some constructive support would have been helpful.

Her confidence was reaffirmed on a rather mild February afternoon when Malcolm entered her office, shut the door, and sat down without making a sound. He plopped a manila folder on her desk and leaned back into the chair.

"I've got the perfect thing to get you past Poulfry," he said.

"Malcolm, I'm…" she began.

"Open the file, Makayla. It's time for the company to move forward with our first *step three*. We've got to start somewhere, and I think this is perfect for us and for you. Please breathe. I skipped the company CPR training, so I'd probably just end up tonguing a corpse. There you go."

She stared at the folder. She was repulsed by what it meant and by what she would become if she opened it. But she was also mortified at what it would mean to reject Malcolm Spier. This man's mind was comfortable with planning and potentially killing the once rich and famous, so why would he be disturbed at ending her pointless life? She reached for the folder, and just as her fingers made contact, she flinched.

"Listen. What happened to Nate wasn't your fault, but this," he reached out and tapped the folder, "this will be."

He moved the folder across her desk, and Makayla's hand made the decision that her brain could not.

"In that folder you'll find the unfinished work of our former colleague, Jimmy Larkin. Don't worry if you can't picture him – I don't think you two spent much time together after your orientation. He was working on a rather light acquisition named Nicholas Seitz. Oh, that rings a bell, huh? Well, this washout was pretty much cleaned up and ready for his television debut when Larkin surprised me with his resignation letter."

"Did he know about your new system, Malcolm?"

"I know you mean *our* new system, and no, Jimmy had no idea where we're taking this company. Anyway, I was looking through his progress with Seitz, and I was damn excited to see that steps one and two were completed.

While he wasn't able to get all of Seitz's eighties hits, Larkin was able to secure the exclusive rights to his comeback adventure. The little bastard was also pretty inventive in getting Seitz back into the mainstream. Open to page three or four. You see that? He recorded every gig Seitz performed, every interview he gave, and every thought that came out of his head, and then put it all on the Web. The videos are damn popular, and interest is growing. Larkin even had him booked on one of those morning shows next month."

"It all sounds great," she said.

"This will be a perfect trial for you. You've got the touring and business experience from Poulfry and the direction and guidance from Charlie and me. What I want you to do on your own is figure out how Nick Seitz will exit this world. If you can do this, if you can put every piece of this method together, I will give you a true partner's cut and the privilege of overseeing Pearle Collier's goodbye tour and Everett Beechum's rise to fame."

He left her office without her response. She flipped back to the first page of Larkin's file (something she'd have to destroy as soon as she'd memorized it) and began reading about Seitz.

Seitz had been one of the loudest screeching, highest kicking, hardest partying frontmen of the eighties, and should have become one of the most revered vocalists in Rock history. What he became, though, was a punchline for every DJ, VJ, and talk show host. After three platinum albums, countless gallons of vodka, and miles worth of cocaine, he decided to break up his band, ApocLips, and pursue a solo career in the emerging grunge scene. His laughably simple lyrics about sex and teenage rebellion had been perfect for entertaining stadiums full of teased-hair fans, but the seriousness of the Seattle music movement had left him embarrassed after concerts, ridiculed by the diehard fans, and, after only a few years, devoid of friends, followers, and money...

Makayla stopped reading and closed the folder. This all sounded too familiar, too close to what she had seen, in terms of the decline in fortune and fame, with Nate. She placed the file in her desk and decided that the less she knew about Seitz, and the farther she stayed from him, the easier her job would be.

"How the hell am I going to do this?" she uttered.

As she sat back in her chair, her mind turned to her love, Alexis, and her neglected father. She couldn't understand the affection she had toward this woman, but she was smart enough not to question it. What she wasn't able to explain, however, were her feelings of guilt over her father's situation. In no way had she caused their fractured relationship or his destroyed marriage, but ever since their last visit she had felt a driving desire to take control of the situation and to make his remaining time on earth tolerable. With the money she was making off her salary and Poulfry, she and Alexis had been able to find a larger apartment and with their combined funds, Makayla would soon be able to get her father out of his hospital, move him to New York, and have Alexis become his homecare nurse. It wouldn't cost them any money in care expenses, thanks to his VA coverage, and he would be able to die comfortably, surrounded by those who loved him.

Makayla pondered these things and decided that she needed to get away from her office and her new file. She left everything but her coat and went home for the evening.

X

Makayla actually couldn't wait to get home. Their new apartment still felt like a hotel suite, but it was in a slightly more refined area in Brooklyn, and the thought of having her father, even if he was little more than a wax statue, near her was comforting. At this particular moment, however, on what should have been a refreshing walk home, every rational part of her conscience ripped and fought to defend itself against the possibility of breaking one of the most sacred commandments. She needed the reassurance, support, and guidance that only a loved one can provide. She had abstained from religious followings, but, whether she realized it or not, her moral groundings were derived from amalgamations of the teachings of Moses, Jesus, Gloria Steinem, Buddha, and Mohammed. Like everything else for her millennial generation, morality and religion had been organized into a convenient playlist.

The air and exercise did nothing to relieve her. She bumped back and forth with the other walking workers and kept her focus on the ground. She had long ago stopped apologizing for any accidental contact, and today she was getting aggravated at the public's lack of manners and nonchalant violence. She didn't acknowledge her own role as aggressor, but what she did begin to feel was simple and blinding rage.

"Assholes," she said as she left the crowd and entered the subway stairs.

She leaned against the walls with her headphones in.

Nothing was playing, but she didn't want to solve any lost tourist's problems or bullshit an answer about the train schedule or accept a compliment for her outfit. At this moment, she wanted to be angry and alone.

She didn't know why, but she began to think about the meeting she had had with Malcolm and Charlie after the vigil for Poulfry. They had secluded themselves in Malcolm's office and began plotting out Spier Records and Entertainment's new direction. Makayla had actually felt guilty at how enthusiastic she had been during this murder/manslaughter educational seminar. Something cult-like had transpired; they were feeding off one another's sick ideas, joking and behaving as if the victims would be fictitious characters in a movie or players in a scene, but the results of this professional development would be very deadly. The process ended with every mark being erased from the vintage chalkboard Malcolm had in his office; no physical traces of their scheme could be left. The developed steps were simple enough to remember and pass on to those worthy of knowing. It roughly reduced to this: each of the company's clients would have a carefully crafted comeback-marketing strategy, and an even more meticulously planned curtain call, specifically tailored to each artist's past drug, alcohol, or sexual habits. Extensive research would have to be done to uncover any past or current mental health issues; if any physical or psychological stressors were identified, Makayla and the other talent scouts would subtly exploit them until organs or psyches ruptured. All three had agreed that the ideal artists would be ones who voluntarily exited, but if they proved to be too fond of their lives and fame, SR&E would turn to the old reliables: overdoses, self (with assistance) inflicted gunshot wounds, asphyxiations, heart attacks, or car accidents. Malcolm had thought that they might have to fill the ranks with some new amoral talent scouts, and filling those positions wouldn't be overly difficult. Being in this business for fifty years had put him in contact with some lurid characters, but he withheld making this final call, for bringing in more people meant more coordinating, more salaries to pay, and higher chances of betrayal.

After figuring out a rough path for their talents' departures, the three crafted the most important part of the new step: public relations. They had determined that notifying the world of their stars' deaths had to be controlled through social media rumors and salacious alerts. When possible, death notices should immediately be sent to the dregs of the dot-coms like *celebdirrt* and *hacks-and-leaks*. Timing really would be essential with these releases. Too early and the wrong suspicions might be piqued. Too late and the carefully crafted story risked being distorted. To balance the tabloid coverage, SR&E would also send releases to the respectable press. Controlling the narrative from both perspectives would be essential. The information golem would feed insatiably off the fingers and screens of the celebrity obsessed public, and memorabilia sales would soar. The entire process would take months to execute, so they would have to employ an incredibly diverse client base.

Makayla thought about that afternoon as she rode her train to Brooklyn and wondered what she would do about Seitz. She hadn't read that much of Larkin's file, but her phone now told her that Seitz was sober, happily divorced, and particularly vain. The stories of his narcissism could not have been real. They must have been the exaggerations of over-enthused bloggers and paparazzi, she thought, but after searching several (apparently) valid sources, she discovered that he had delayed performances because he had been staring into his dressing room mirror, blowing himself kisses and reciting motivational speeches. She especially liked this one: at every show, he had demanded that he screen any potential groupie.

Despite her disgust, she laughed as she read. By the time she reached her stop, her anger had subsided; ironically enough, her job had calmed her down.

XI

Makayla's first meeting with Nick Seitz had occurred only hours before his morning talk show appearance. Their introduction had been scheduled a week earlier, but Seitz had not taken the news of Jimmy Larkin's exit very well. Initially, he had hung up on her. He had then called back to curse out Malcolm. With his forked tongue, Malcolm was able to convince the washed-up singer that Makayla was much more experienced and qualified than Larkin had ever been. Before Seitz could object, Malcolm quickly told him that it had been Makayla who had resurrected Nate Poulfry's dismal career, and when Seitz heard this, his tone had changed from acerbic to apathetic.

Makayla didn't see spending less time with Seitz as a loss. After the mildly successful interview and performance had ended, she left to get something to eat, and he exited, without explanation, in a cab. After an hour or so, he had sent her a message that was as close to a compliment as she'd ever get from him, but she didn't mind. A short while after that text, she had received a message about keeping up to date with his online image and that he'd be in touch. This message had actually made her feel more comfortable because she was determined to associate with him from a distance, as a butcher would with his animals. His online image, in fact, was going to be Makayla's focus; she would mold him into what his former fans wanted to see. She would create a new artist who was fully remorseful for breaking up ApocLips; a new artist who had realized the error of his arrogance, and a new man who was older and wiser and ready to entertain a new generation.

I just hope this group of kids buys into his music like they do eighties fashion, she mused.

When she got back to her office, she began working on every social media outlet she could think of. She spent hours posting videos, writing messages, and commenting on blogs, and, before leaving for home, she went to see Malcolm.

"He's no Nate, Malcolm."

"He doesn't have to be, darlin'. All he has to be is valuable. I've been checking the site that Larkin set up and it's racking up more and more views each day. With this morning's performance, which was actually very good, we should be able to start recording his new album within the month."

"He's written an entire album already?"

"Not at all. Larkin had convinced him to reinterpret his nineties solo work. Didn't you read the file?"

She glanced down in embarrassment.

"It would be just as well that you take a little more time with Seitz."

"Why's that?"

"I got a rather long email from an old friend of mine. He tells me that Pearle Collier will need quite a bit more time before she's ready for her final performance. Apparently she's got a few polyps on her vocal cords that will require surgery, and while it's a minor procedure, she's going to need a bit before she's confident in her voice. This pushes back a few of my larger plans, maybe by a year or so, but things are still looking good for us."

"It certainly looks like it."

"Do me a favor and read the damn file," he said and turned back to his computer screen.

She would read the file when she got home, and

she would also make a very important phone call to her friend and former roommate. She had stopped listening to Malcolm after she had heard him say "Surgery", for she had had her own morbid epiphany.

"You have a beautiful smile," said a fellow straphanger.

She hadn't realized she had been. She thanked the man and looked down to her purse, shuffling things around to avoid any real conversation.

When she arrived at the apartment, she found a note from Alexis. She thought it was cute how her sweetie had refused to give up the classic paper messages. Makayla's eyes widened when she read that her father could be moved to their apartment by early March. In her elation, she let out a celebratory scream, and danced around as she preheated the oven and prepared her dinner. As the cutlets reheated, she took out her phone and dialed her friend, JiHae Liu.

The conversation lasted longer than Makayla had intended, but after quite a bit of cajoling she was able to get the information she needed. JiHae was a novice in the medical field, but her mother, Mrs. Liu, was a renowned surgeon who knew the best and worst names in reconstructive surgery. Makayla explained to Ji that SR&E needed to establish several steady relationships with reasonably priced plastic surgeons because their new clientele might be encouraged to transform their images. Makayla offered the broadest outline of her company's business model, and Ji promised to put her extremely busy mother in contact with Makayla. The conversation finished with thank yous and empty promises to meet up for drinks.

Makayla fixed her now burned dinner and thought about how she'd spend the lonely night. Alexis was working an overnight shift, and Makayla didn't feel like reading or watching TV. She was weighing her other options when her phone rang. She didn't recognize the number but decided to pick up; it could have been Seitz, or something related to him.

"Hello."

"Is this Makayla?" a woman asked.

"It is, but who…"

"This is JiHae's mother, Dr. Liu. I just got her text and, honestly, this is the only free time I've got today, so let me give you the names of some of my reputable colleagues."

"Thank you, Mrs. Liu, but I don't know if Ji explained how tight my company's budget is right now. This type of procedure would obviously be paid for out of our pockets, so I need some decent yet very reasonably priced doctors."

"Then why don't you take your names from subway ads?"

"Because I'm looking for someone who keeps quiet about who they're working on. I need someone who will work at extremely short notice and then stay quiet about the job. If that means using someone who doesn't exactly have the best record or who isn't known by every commuter in the city, so be it."

"If that's the case, I'll have to call you back. The names I have are not what you're looking for. I'll be in touch with you by the end of the week – I have to find out if the doctor I'm thinking about is still allowed to practice."

"Thank you, Mrs. Liu. I really appreciate it."

"Good night, Makayla."

Not only was the doctor still allowed to practice (even after having been held civilly liable for the deaths of two patients) but he was willing to work with Makayla outside the bounds of his daily practice. She contacted him just after Dr. Liu had called back, and after several days of phone tag and rather intense negotiations, she had accepted an exorbitant rate for Nick Seitz's upcoming facelift. All she had to do now was convince Seitz that he needed one. Her first step, in a about month or so, after his popularity had grown to a more lucrative point, would be to attack him on his website and on social media. She would systematically unleash a tirade of insults and jokes about his sagging jowls, his wrinkled forehead, and his jiggling turkey neck. She would then turn to her *Wittier* account and start a campaign to ridicule his performances, interviews, and albums. She knew that Seitz, as arrogant as he was, was also incredibly fragile where his image was concerned. He wouldn't be able to handle another public backlash against his career, so he'd turn to her and Malcolm for help. Makayla would be the first to suggest the plastic surgery, and Malcolm would surely support her opinion.

She decided that it was time to enlighten Malcolm about her third step plan for Nicholas Seitz.

XII

By early summer Makayla's father had settled into his new apartment and routine, and Nick Seitz's comeback tour had erupted. His performances had sold out and his newly released album was doing very well. He had even begun to accept Makayla as a professional. This pleased her, not because she cared about his opinions or approval, but because earning his trust was integral to her plan.

She had been waiting for him to open up to her. Finally he had asked her advice about the constant online attacks on his looks and age, and she had steered him toward the idea of plastic surgery. At first he had been hesitant, but she had convinced him that SR&E had a reputable surgeon on call for situations like this.

Just after his Fourth of July concert, Nick Seitz went to have his face sliced apart, stretched out, and stitched back together. What he did not know was that Makayla, with Malcolm's blessing and money, had paid the surgeon an extra 25,000 dollars to make sure Seitz never woke up. Makayla had penned the doctor's excuse herself.

Nicholas Seitz's death could only be described as a tragic accident. According to Makayla's note, and the doctor's lawyer, Seitz's years of drug abuse had left his heart incapable of handling the anesthesia. Meanwhile, Makayla and SR&E successfully went on to coordinate their own nostalgia campaign for the former ApocLips frontman.

XIII

By the late fall, Pearle Collier had recovered from her minor procedure and had traveled to New York with her nephew and Sylvan Thoreau. She had started her studio sessions off slowly, but even her recovering voice was one of the strongest Andres Marr had ever heard.

"How does that sound, Mr. Marr?"

Pearle Collier asked the question out of pure politeness. Spending the majority of her life in recording studios, repeatedly singing verses, choruses, and solos had given her as good an ear as any producer could hope to have. Even after all these years, she was a professional who believed that every person in the process was valuable and deserving of respect. She was also aware that her voice, while still remarkable, was aging along with every other muscle and joint in her body. She was carrying a bit more weight, mostly in her voluminous breasts, but her lithe and graceful movements matched her angelic voice. This was her first time back in a studio in many, many years. Yes, she had performed a few years ago at Saul Sildon's tribute concert, but she had considered it a personal embarrassment. She hadn't properly warmed her voice before the show, and decided to sing an octave below the original notes in the three selected songs, but the audience either didn't realize the alteration or didn't care. They applauded and stood after each of her appearances.

"Ms. Collier…"

"Call me Pearle, darling."

"It's an honor to be in the same room with you, Pearle. For the first take, you sounded amazing, but you were a bit flat going into the bridge, and I think our choice of dropping down was a good one. When you're ready, we'll start from '…thinking it's the right time' and then listen through the playback."

Andres Marr was a Grammy Award winning producer whose abilities had been squandered on pampered talentless pop stars. His job had evolved from music producer to waste manager and voice tuner. Most of the singers he had recently recorded came full of the indulgent diva mentality but only had the talent of a small-town high school star. In his opinion, the archetype for these vessels had been Rita Symone. He had produced her final album, a record that had been heavily marketed to convince her critics that she actually possessed a legitimate singing voice. She did not. What she did have was an army of publicists, a dancer's physique, a copious assortment of designer clothes, hordes of makeup artists, and a magician in the studio. The sessions had lasted for weeks. The requests from Symone and her entourage spanned from the annoying to the absurd, and when it was finally finished, she still sounded, at best, like a high pitched shriek filtered through an intercom. The damn album, even in the days of Musiikki, went platinum. When he read about her death, he was sad for the loss of the beautiful woman but hopeful that her absence would make room for more musically inclined stars. With Rita Symone as a memory, her generation would have to take another step toward responsibility and adulthood, and a younger group would have the opportunity to create on an artistically clean canvas.

"When do my Oysters arrive?" Pearle asked through her microphone.

"We've got another two hours, Ms. – Pearle," he responded.

"How about we break for some lunch before then?"

"Sounds great. I'll see you back here at one o'clock."

Malcolm had been correct in his assessment of the remaining Oysters being easy to locate; his interns were able to find them after a few online searches and a handful of phone calls. Terry Jones (second generation), Olivia Wallace (original), Charlotte Winfeld (original), and Harriet Wilcott (third generation) were somewhat hesitant, but ultimately agreed to Spier's proposal. Each would receive studio time with Marr and Pearle, a wardrobe allowance, a free hotel suite, and a generous sum of 5,000 each for their reunion performance at Carnegie Hall. Malcolm was coupling Pearle's performance with a tribute to Poulfry during the rather lackadaisical March/April tourist months. This was the only time the venue could offer, and the hall's management was very pleased with the timing and lineup. Malcolm was able to acquire many of Poulfry's contemporary artists, both musicians and actors, to cover his songs and narrate clips from the upcoming documentary. Poulfry's portion would open the night – a mourning of his death – and Pearle Collier and The Oysters would be the quintessential celebration of life. He hoped that closing with Collier would focus the public's attention toward her past and present careers and away from the loss of Nate. Sales of his merchandise and music had begun to plateau anyway. Before any type of show could be produced, however, Malcolm had to make sure that The Oysters were able to support, as they had once brilliantly done, Pearle's voice and personality. Marr understood the task, and he was quite adept at maneuvering and facilitating egos, jealousy, and, if it existed between the women, years' worth of simmering resentment. To his pleasant amazement, though, he did not have to expend any energy at quelling arguments or soothing damaged personalities. The elderly women arrived in the lobby of the studio (several cushioned chairs just outside of the booths, really) and were prepared to get down to work. Each greeted Andres with a smile and a feigned nervousness about recording their classics. It had been decades since they sang together, but all were still confident in their own capabilities. It was a confidence that both the gifted ladies and the demented shared – the former were too old to give a shit about opinions, and the latter just couldn't comprehend the notions of praise and reverence. Whatever their reasons were, the ladies seemed magnanimous and ready for one last moment of fame. When Pearle arrived back from her lunch with Sylvan, the group paused for an awkward few seconds and then reunited like sorority sisters. From his booth, Marr smiled at the scene, clicked the mic, and asked the women if they were ready to work. They politely ignored him for a few more laughs, and then Pearle responded.

"Mr. Marr, let's see what these ole mammies can do."

They exploded with laughter and threw their own sisterly insults back at Pearle. Marr laughed in his booth and continued to relax. Money was being lost as the minutes passed by, but interrupting this joyous display was simply not going to happen. They went through some vocal warm-ups, poked fun at one another while doing so, and then moved to their respective spots. When they began singing *Anna's Bells*, Andres Marr made a few subtle adjustments on his board, removed his hands, put them behind his head, and absorbed the most perfect voices he'd ever heard.

XIV

Makayla unwound her scarf and unlocked the apartment door. What she wanted to see was her lover wearing a stethoscope and little else, but what she got was her buck-naked father running through the living room, bleeding from his left hand, Alexis in tow with a syringe in hand.

"At ease, Sergeant!" she screamed.

Alexis had discovered that barking orders as if he were still in the service was incredibly effective. Regardless of how deteriorated his brain was, his military conditioning still governed most of his behavior. It didn't stop him in this instance, though. When Makayla stepped in, he turned his head just quickly enough to stumble over their rustically styled coffee table. He was scrambling to get back to his stride when Alexis plunged the needle into the blackness of his ass. After a few moments of being restrained he was pacified, and Alexis and Makayla hoisted him from the floor, dressed him in his pajamas, and put him down for a nap.

Makayla unpacked their dinner and heated it in the microwave while Alexis set their eat-in kitchen table. When Makayla sat down with two glasses of wine, Alexis told her some very obvious news.

"As beautiful as you are, you look like shit."

Makayla ignored the comment in order to buy time for the conversation she didn't want to have; it isn't every day you present a murder proposal to your girlfriend. Instead of the truth, she changed the subject.

"My dad still busting your balls because you're white?"

"May, he's getting to the point where I could be Martian green. You still care that I'm white?" she asked seductively over the rim of her wine glass.

Makayla figured that this was as good a sexual segue as she'd ever heard. They left their dinner to cool and stripped one another all the way to the shower.

As they lay in bed, Makayla asked Alexis if there were certain triggers that might spur her father's memories. Alexis explained that each case of dementia was different, that each person would have moments of clarity brought on by certain motions, touches, scents, songs, etc., but finding one that would consistently work was difficult at best. When Makayla heard the suggestion of music, she quickly recalled his experience with the MÜS when she had visited the VA. She decided in that instant that her father and girlfriend would be her honored guests at Pearle Collier's reunion show. Alexis thought that bringing Jordan was an excellent idea; she had been taking him for daily walks and trips around the city, and aside from a few outbursts at the costumed characters in Times Square, she concluded that it had been an incredibly successful experiment. She was an ardent believer in the philosophy that dementia sufferers needed stimulation and pleasure, not controlled confinement and medication. This inspiration had come from early in her career when she studied several European institutions that had erected facilities mimicking small suburban communities. Most of them had functioning retail shops, restaurants, movie theaters, ice-cream parlors, and libraries. While she didn't have the safety of an artificial campus, Alexis was able to escort Jordan through the real city when the multitudes had settled into their destinations. He seemed to enjoy the time out, the crisp air, and if there were any serious behavioral issues, she had her syringe in her purse.

"Now would you please tell me why you came home looking like someone you loved died?" Alexis asked.

Makayla was hoping that she had let it go. "Always the caregiver, huh?" she responded.

"I consider myself as just a plain giver," Alexis said, moving closer, kissing Makayla's neck. She made two circuits from below the ear to the clavicle and then continued her inquiry.

"I saw you when you were depressed, May. After we got back from Cristol, I was really worried about you – even thought about calling Malcolm's personal doctor – but the look on your face when you came through that door tonight truly frightened me. Granted it was only for the split second before I had to tackle your father, but my job is to assess patients and heal them as best I can. Tell me what's going on."

Makayla stared at her for a few moments before dropping her eyes, and Alexis reflexively jerked her head backwards. This conversation was sending Makayla from a dark pit to a glacial crevice of despair. If Alexis were aware of any part of Malcolm's plans, she would be complicit, at the very least, in murder, but Makayla knew that the subject would not be dropped or diverted.

"Malcolm gave me a new assignment, and I don't know if what the hell I'm going to do with it yet. This musician, Everett Beechum, is talented, very talented, but I'd have to bring him up, coordinate the publicity, book shows with venues that expect known names, oversee recording sessions, and book an entirely new tour. I still don't know enough about this shit to start from scratch with an unknown name!" she lied convincingly.

She had worked up some anxious tears and a slight drip from her left nostril. Alexis reached with her left arm and plucked two tissues from the box. She placed them in Makayla's hands and sat up against the headboard. She gently guided her girlfriend's sobbing head to her bare chest and put her own chin down into the fluffy mass of curly black hair.

As Makayla was dozing off on Alexis's chest, Malcolm, about twenty miles to the east, sat in the newly refurbished memorabilia room of his Manhasset Hills home. He sat in his favorite recliner, strumming the signed Poulfry acoustic and sipping a North Fork Cabernet. The room wasn't quite finished, but the built-in shelves and lighting would be done before the holidays. He had roughly planned the room to fit at least ten displays, but the only three labels and pictures that he had hung so far were those of Nate Poulfry, Nick Seitz, and Pearle Collier. His conscience was in no way disturbed. He felt a bit lonely, but not guilty; he hadn't done anything to bring on remorse or shame. Nate had killed himself, and the Pearle Collier everyone remembered and adored had died years ago. In a way, he mused, he wouldn't be killing anyone; from his perspective, he'd be reviving her heyday-self in a murderous reverse séance. What he was meditating on, as he strummed through the five or six songs he knew by heart, was how they would actually kill the old R&B singer. She had never dabbled with drugs, was extremely private and old fashioned with her love life (Sylvan had always said more than he should), didn't have enemies who would go to such an extreme as murder, and she didn't take part in any dangerous or excessive extracurricular activities. He poured the remnants of the award winning 2008 into his glass as his mind filtered through the greatest killers in history, literature, and film. Most, real and fictional, had been caught. He didn't care for that fact. He wasn't a sadist looking to reap pleasure from torture and pain, he was a businessman looking to make money off of quiet deaths. He took a sip of his wine, placed the guitar on its wall mount, picked up his phone, and made a call to one of his favorite services. He carefully listened to his options. Maybe clearing his head(s) would help him think.

He could get used to being right. For the fleeting few moments of clarity he gained, her services had been worth every thousand. He strode through his cavernous house with his robe open and slippers loudly flopping. Only a scant few lights illuminated the halls, yet they seemed to cast an angelic glow on his hairless scalp. He had finally figured it out. He wouldn't call this idea an epiphany exactly, but it would solve a very many variables in his plan. He would inform Charlie and Makayla first thing tomorrow morning.

Makayla was in charge of the coffee for the morning meeting. Malcolm had left three voicemails (he refused to text) about the urgency of this dawn assembly, jabbering through her earpiece but not giving any clues to the source of his ecstasy. He simply insisted that she be in his office by seven and that she pick up the Java. She opened the door to her old café and relished in the wafts of the roasted grinding beans. They offered many varieties, all organic and certified fair trade, and all were moderately priced for the city. She didn't recognize the barista behind the frother, but she smiled politely and ordered three large black coffees to go. He seemed to appreciate the simple order with a smile that said "Thank you" and turned around to pour her order. As she slid her purse from her hip to her ribs, she caught sight of Café Tierra's music rack and froze. The small rustic shelf was only a couple of feet high, but its bottom two racks were filled with Nate Poulfry's recently-recorded final show, *Live in*

Cristol. Her eyes moved up the shelves as if scanning her Tetris pile and saw a rack with only one remaining CD. On it was the newly remastered Pearle Collier album, *My Baby's Ride.*

"That will be twelve eighty-seven, Ma'am," said the tattooed barista.

Makayla turned and handed him her debit card. As he swiped it, she twirled back to study the shelf. Her closer scrutiny revealed the faux fall foliage festooning the stand's perimeter. It was nestled between several small bales of hay, and on a sandwich board prices were creatively sketched in colored chalk.

"Like a receipt?" he asked.

"No, that's all right," she responded. "Guess Poulfry's not as popular as he once was," she added, indicating the rack.

"Actually, I had a chance to restock it – just before you came in. I've got more of the other one back here, too. *Pollyay* or something. I've never heard of her, but people have been buying both for weeks. Didn't think the brick and mortar market existed for music anymore, and I definitely didn't think anyone used CDs anymore, but I guess there's still a generation who doesn't know how to rip this stuff offline."

He handed her the order in a nifty cardboard carrier and thanked her for the business. She reciprocated the thank you for his service and made her way to the door. She couldn't understand her reaction: she had grown up buying CDs, then burning copies of those albums with her friends, and later converting the enormous troves into MP3s and playlists to satisfy all the facets of her busy life. She had always been the avaricious consumer, but had never played a role in producing a tangible product. Now, here in her old coffee shop, sat the fruits of her sweat, labor, and tears. There, on what looked like an antique rack, sat Nate Poulfry's immortality, and she had helped create it. Just before she exited into the brisk early-December coldness, she pivoted on the ball of her left foot, walked directly to the rack, and went back to the register with *Live in Cristol* in hand. As she passed it over to be scanned, she saw her name on the back credits. Next to the title, Producer, appeared, in a tiny Arial font, **Makayla Rogers**. She carefully placed the album in her purse, and with a foreign sense of pride and accomplishment, headed for the office.

Malcolm watched Makayla walk into his office and saw something different in her posture: this was a different employee. She was moving rhythmically, confidently, and with a purpose. This was the woman he had once hoped of meeting. He pushed the chair from his desk and stood to help her with the coffee.

"You don't look like you need one of these," he said as he put the coffees on his desk. "You look like you're coming from the best lay of your life. Sorry, no pun intended," he added with a grin.

"This is some seriously good fucking coffee, Malcolm. And this is a seriously amazing fucking record," she said as she liberated the CD from her purse.

The crinkling plastic reminded him of the foil condom wrapper he had fumbled with the night before, and he let out a loud laugh.

"That one is entirely your success. You didn't pay for that, did you? You know I inter-officed a copy to you when we first released it, right?"

Her victorious smile turned to one of innocent embarrassment, and Malcolm laughed louder and heartier. Instead of having organized that large mountain of mail that had accrued in her office, she had just thrown everything away.

Before she could attempt to cover up her mistake, Charlie flew through the door like Nor'easter's gust and demanded his caffeine. He threw his jacket onto the rack and skipped the professional courtesies.

"What's so damn funny, and why the hell are we here at dawn, Malcolm?"

"Sit down, sit down, both of you," Malcolm responded, still chuckling. "We're here because I've finally figured out how Ms. Collier will take us into a new tax bracket."

Makayla and Charlie settled into their seats as Malcolm closed the door.

Could it actually work? She was skeptical – very skeptical – but she also felt more confident in Malcolm and herself than she ever had. Sitting at her desk, now half past ten, she grew angry at her initial doubt; she had followed doubt her entire life and it had led her to little more than anxiety. Her new skin and shell had the potential of being filled with confidence and success, but she first needed guidance and direction. She was entirely ready to erase nearly thirty years of self-destructive thought processing, but it would not happen after buying a single CD, nor would it happen after premeditating a single homicide. She leaned back in her chair and thought about anyone, someone more personally connected to her than Malcolm, she might consider as an idol of confidence and strength. She thought of her father, but surviving through dementia wasn't noble – perhaps it was for the caretaker, but not for the patient. She thought of her friend and former roommate, JiHae, who had stoically persevered through med school and a grueling residency without throwing herself of CNYU's roof, but had done so more for the approval of her parents than for her own satisfaction. Parents. She hadn't thought about the other half of her own parental equation in months. Her mother had, as plainly as can be described, abandoned her daughter, her husband, and her own life. Makayla pondered this scenario for a moment and arrived at a mature conclusion: instead of reacting to her mother with selfish rage, she forced herself to analyze things through a clear neutral lens as opposed to the view of a scared, isolated little girl. Yes, Etta had left them, but she hadn't done so until she was certain Makayla had dedicated herself to graduate school. She also hadn't left her husband to rot in his own solitary prison. No. Through this new scope, Makayla began to understand that her mother had found, whether spurred by frustration or mortality, the nerve to go out and find the freedom, independence, and confidence that her daughter now ardently sought. Makayla brought the chair to its completely upright position and picked up her still sealed Poulfry CD.

"Where in the world is Etta C. Rogers?" she sang to the tune of one of her favorite childhood TV shows.

She let the CD case flop onto her desk and made a mental note to backtrack through her mother's messages and postcards when she got home. She then switched her focus to the buzzing alarm emanating from her phone. She had completely forgotten about meeting Everett Beechum and Sylvan Thoreau for the band auditions. They were still in need of a guitarist, a bassist, a percussionist, and at least three violinists to round out the supporting band. Beechum would be alternating between saxophone, trombone, trumpet, and piano (depending what the song called for), and he had been very helpful in suggesting musicians for the auditions. The names he had provided were not well known to the general public, but that made them readily available, highly adaptable, and relatively cheap. He had avidly vouched for their talents, and Malcolm had vouched for Everett's, so she decided to trust his judgment. She killed the alarm, grabbed what she needed, and left for the studio. Malcolm was using his newest gadget, his hands-free adaptor, and as she passed by his office, she looped her scarf around her neck, waved, and mouthed a goodbye. For some absurd reason, perhaps influenced by his favorite spy thrillers, he always pressed one finger against the earpiece as he spoke, as if the pressure helped transmit his call, and instead of politely waving back to his protégé, he threw his free hand at her like a fatigued boxer, turned his back, and spoke louder to the phantom on the other end. She finished the knot in her scarf and decided to react as her new, confident self as opposed to the meek, meager girl who would have spent the afternoon contemplating the myriad meanings of his rude gesture; she tilted her chin up a bit higher and basked in this new persona. She looked forward to the day when there would be no internal divide between the old and the new Makayla Rogers; she reveled in the idea that soon there would be only the one assertive woman.

The initial auditions were not scheduled to last for too long – in fact, they weren't planned to go past a first round, so even calling them auditions was a misnomer. Those who were arriving today, unless grossly incompetent or completely unreliable, were going to be suited up and staged behind Pearle Collier and The Oysters in just over three months. It seemed like a narrow window to mount such a major production, but the majority of these musicians were seasoned professionals, and Malcolm and his new underlings were covering the Poulfry tribute portion of the evening. She met Everett and Sylvan at Leute Geists. The owner was very appreciative of the uptick in business since Malcolm had introduced himself, and had opened the club exclusively for today's viewings and several of the upcoming rehearsals. Pearle and The Oysters didn't exactly fit the venue's demographics, but these would be closed virtually private sessions. The stars insisted on zero publicity until they were confident in their voices and sound. Makayla had assured Sylvan that no one outside of the club's owner and small staff would know where the group was rehearsing. She failed to mention to Sylvan that Malcolm had already made some calls to his old allies in the paparazzi and she was busy unleashing a subtle barrage of rumors in the social media realm.

"Ms. Rogers?" Sylvan asked as Makayla slipped through the door.

"Mr. Thoreau, I presume," she said with confidence and zeal.

"My gosh. Malcolm wasn't lying. Please forgive me if I'm being rude, but I'm too old to hold back my tongue. You are radiant."

She took absolutely no offense, and was honestly flattered, because as he was apologizing for his lack of propriety, he was kissing her hand and bowing as low as his old joints would permit. The stories she had heard from Malcolm were instantly vindicated by Sylvan's old fashioned charm and seemingly genial nature.

"Pearle – she will insist that you call her Pearle, and please call me Sylvan – is in the restroom. She always likes to get a feel for a venue and its acoustics, even if it's just a rehearsal, before she starts working. We've been here for about an hour or so. She can't wait to get started, and I haven't felt this giddy in years."

As Makayla was about to speak, Pearle Collier emerged from the back of club, dressed casually but with obvious care and dignity. She walked toward Sylvan, and when she saw Makayla she smiled brightly and accelerated her steps. She took both of the young producer's hands into her own and looked directly into those beautiful eyes. The new Assertive Makayla remained in place, but something else very interesting occurred for the briefest of moments. Makayla, with Pearle's two gestures which she had interpreted as maternal, was flung twenty years into the past. She was looking at her mother's doppelgänger. The almond colored skin, the full lips, the high cheek bones, the carefully styled greying hair, and the plumpness which haunts elderly women were all in proportion to the memory of Etta Rogers. Before the moment of staring became too awkward, Makayla was able to stammer out her greeting.

"Ms. Collier, I can't tell you what an honor it is to meet you. I'm sorry, Pearle, Sylvan told me, and I'm sorry for staring at you like I was going to take a bite, but you remind me so much of my mother."

"Oh, I'm so sorry, dear. When did she pass?"

"No, no, no, she's not dead. She's just disappeared to travel the world, leaving me to take care of my father. Well, not at first, but…I was actually going to try and catch up with her later, but look, I'm babbling, so when you're ready, we'll get started."

Pearle was very happy with this young woman. There seemed to be sincerity in her words, authority in the way she directed the room and its people, and an honest passion in the work she was doing. Pearle watched Makayla throughout the day and observed the way she spoke to the artists, listened to the questions they asked, and was satisfied with the professional critiques she made. Makayla was still a cub in this business, but touring and working with Poulfry and Seitz had apparently seasoned her very quickly. Pearle was no believer in the cult of positive thinking, but she was always impressed at how constructive critiques from those in authority seemed to beget success and assuredness in those who were performing. Makayla also impressed Sylvan, a man who had seen every type of producer over his career. She was not averse to telling the musicians to play louder at times, or asking them to explain their technique at others, or letting them play uninterrupted. She also put them at ease by not demanding they acknowledge her role as the lord over their careers. They knew what kind of an opportunity this was for their futures and they recognized that she held the key to their passages to greater things, but she never once used this for her own leverage. With her relaxed, professional aura, they were able to express why they deserved the chance to play with the iconic Pearle Collier and The Oysters. They had no clue that Makayla wasn't watching anyone else today, or ever, for this show, so she didn't have to be nervous about making any life-altering decisions.

As the session ended, Makayla stood on the stage and asked everyone to take a seat before her. She pulled out the drummer's stool and sat comfortably as she made her closing announcement.

"Ladies and gentlemen…" She waited until it was silent, then resumed. "Our work for Pearle Collier's comeback show at Carnegie Hall will begin next Wednesday promptly at nine in the morning. We have to take complete advantage of this space and time, because after the holiday spirit drains the city dry, we will begin setting up and rehearsing at the hall five days a week, with weekends as needed. I know the notice is short. I will provide all of the new additions – congratulations, by the way – with SR&E's hotel accommodations. If you'd prefer to find yourself a short-term rental or scour the Web for some kind of share apartment, please feel free, but we have several rooms reserved for the long term at one hotel in the Village and one Uptown. Whatever you decide, please make sure you are ready to work. Our schedule is extraordinarily tight, so if you cannot fulfill your obligations to the group, please let me know immediately. Again, congratulations to the new hires. Please see me at the bar before you leave, you have some paperwork to sign."

Pearle, Sylvan, and Everett began applauding, and were soon joined with celebratory shouts and praises to the Lord. Makayla proudly clapped along with the new group, then made her way to the bar.

XV

The holidays passed rather quietly, aside from the raucous party Malcolm threw for his staff: a bash worthy of old office lore, complete with booze, illicit and prescribed drugs, and the obligatory of-course-it-won't-be-awkward-on-Monday sex. If all of the other seasonal gods were fans of R&B, the deity of winter was not: New York was under siege by one of the coldest, iciest, most snow-filled winters on record. Almost every rehearsal in late January and early February had to be postponed, abbreviated, or canceled. For several days the entire city, save emergency workers who were stuck on double or triple shifts, was completely shut down while storms dropped voluminous amounts of delicately stinging snow. Traveling in any manner was treacherous, and so was being trapped inside buildings where germs and viruses and bacteria were spreading.

One degenerative disease in particular was not reacting well to the constant confinement: Jordan Roger's dementia. There was virtually no safe way to bring him outside, so he remained doubly confined. Alexis immediately observed the growing frustration and changing sleep patterns in her patient, so she consulted with his physician and they agreed to begin a small regime of *Triazalep* to get him to sleep through the night. At first, the cantankerous old man slept as soundly as he had back in boot camp, but after a couple of weeks his patterns began to shift drastically. He continued to sleep soundly, but for only as long as his old drill sergeant used to allow.

He would be awake after a three or four hour burst of rest, and he took to wandering – something he hadn't really done before. On one of his meanderings, he had thoroughly terrified Makayla as she returned home from a late rehearsal. She had staggered in from an ominous howling storm and had high-kneed it up the stairs in an attempt to warm herself. As she pushed open the door, the street light, snow-opaqued and dim, illuminated a bent, bony creature lunging toward the door, screaming, "Etti, you bitch!" Instinctively she backpedaled, but tripped over Alexis's boots and umbrella. She shrieked as she fell squarely on her ass, and was equally embarrassed and relieved when the hallway light illuminated her naked decrepit father.

"Goddammit, soldier, ten-hut!" she bellowed.

At this, he had halted and stood immediately at attention, his testicles and penis still bobbing to the left and right. With the ruckus, Alexis came stumbling out of bed, and commanded the former first sergeant back to his room.

He was becoming more than just one nurse could handle, so Makayla arranged for an alternating nurse three days and nights a week. With Alexis's newfound free time, she was able to get back into a rough exercise routine, sample some of the new neighborhood restaurants with Makayla (when their schedules actually coincided), and what she looked forward to the most was watching Pearle Collier and The Oysters' electrifying rehearsals each Friday. She went as Makayla's date and guest, and was introduced all around. She met Pearle Collier, each Oyster, Everett, his bandmates, and the always charming Sylvan Thoreau. Sylvan instantly reminded Alexis of her uncle Alan, and he seemed to go out of his way to make sure that she felt as if she belonged at the club. She was amazed at how inviting this collection of people was to a total stranger. There was a blatant absence of ego during the rehearsals, and this seemed counterintuitive from everything she had learned from reality TV. With this group, she had no problem, as she usually did when meeting new people, recalling names.

Makayla caught herself watching Alexis as frequently as she watched her group perform. The band and the singers barely needed anything except a morning sound check, which her technician tended to do, meal breaks, which were easy enough for her to call, and decisiveness in calling off rehearsals due to inclement weather. Just as with Poulfry, Makayla's direct role in producing the talent was minimal, and this tour had no travel worked into it.

According to Malcolm's plan, it would be at least another six months to a year after the reunion show before Makayla would have to have any part in the matriarch of gospel's death. He wanted her focusing on mental preparedness; after all, this wasn't some washed-up '80s frontman – this was a music legend. He wanted Makayla to be able to spend months with this woman and her band yet see them as nothing more than livestock. Malcolm had extended the farm and slaughterhouse metaphor to the point where Makayla seriously considered veganism, but she understood his reasoning. Discussing murder was as simple as playing any round of a first person video game shooter, but actually carrying it out would take a nurtured and matured callousness. She had picked up some psychology textbooks to study the minds and methods of serial killers, but they offered little in the way of how-to. She was not a psychopath, and no amount of deranged training would morph her into one. As best as she could determine, psychopaths suffered from an alteration of the brain's chemistry, and she was simply wired properly. In order to function on a daily basis, she decided to procrastinate, a technique she had perfected as an undergrad, and focus on preparing for the upcoming show instead of on the impending crime. So although there weren't many tasks for Makayla to perform at this stage of the plan, she executed them with an air of professionalism and authority that put everyone around her at ease.

Of all the participants and spectators at these rehearsals, no one seemed to be as serene as Sylvan Thoreau. He was delighted to be near his ex-wife again, and she seemed equally ecstatic to be around him. He had never forgotten her voice – it wasn't something that could ever be forgotten – but, like being absent from any sensation for too long, the transformative feeling that it had produced in him had begun to slip away. He was only ever able to compare his physical and emotional response to her singing as a slowly building orgasm – he hadn't forgotten what those felt like either, but he wouldn't naturally experience another one for the rest of his life. He had tried the pills, but his parallel condition, an enlarged prostate, had caused him to dribble piss uncontrollably out of an erection that lasted long past the four hour safety mark. What was equally, and surprisingly, compelling to Sylvan's clouding eyes was seeing the two young lovers, Makayla and Alexis, displaying their relationship as openly as he wished he could have in the beginning with Pearle. The fact that the women were also a mixed couple was a coincidence that filled him with pride. He saw them as the vicarious victory that had eluded his former marriage. He also didn't at all mind that both women were vivacious and lovely; he was incredibly satisfied with this endeavor, regardless of how hostile the winter was.

"All right, everyone," Makayla announced, breaking Sylvan's musing, "the latest report says that this storm is only getting worse, so let's start wrapping up. I'll let you know about tomorrow's schedule later tonight. Please keep your phones on and charged."

She had to repeat that final request for the older crowd. It turned out that the blizzard she had been keeping tabs on shut down rehearsals for the better part of the week. It was also indirectly responsible for Pearle Collier's acute case of walking pneumonia.

Malcolm was becoming very restless with the season he pointedly referred to as Mother Nature's period; he had never had much of a relationship with anything maternal. Storm after storm was crippling both the city and his chances of filling the house for the tribute/reunion show. He thought the real headache would come with booking acts to cover Poulfry's hits, but he had needed to turn at least three older groups away. Even though he was determined to stick to his new business model, he couldn't resist the energy and promise and attractiveness that accompanied youth, so he carefully interspersed four modern acts into Nate's contemporary-heavy lineup. Most of the newer groups, some young enough to be his grandchildren, were extremely talented, but like most artists they struggled to get audiences away from their electronic screens and into concert venues. He was even more pleased that he had persuaded the agents and managers of these sprouting bands to sign exclusive album deals with SR&E. Each band would guarantee Malcolm one record with the option to stay on depending on their sales and fan base. Malcolm maintained the absolute prerogative in making the decision concerning success or failure for each group. They would also receive nothing for playing the show. Out of desperation for international exposure, each agent had agreed to Malcolm's terms and thanked him profusely. Regardless of the weather and his restless mood, Malcolm was in decent spirits.

The only other concern nagging at his mind was how he was supposed to pick up and deliver a van load of homeless vets from their shelters to the Midtown soup kitchen. He didn't mind volunteering – Charlie had informed him that they could craftily hide many of their earnings if they created a non-profit branch for the company and occasionally volunteered to keep it legitimate. Malcolm was dubious at first, mainly because he was shocked that money could be hidden so simply, and secondly because they were getting too busy to spare any employees to humanitarian causes. Like many other things he had doubted in his life, he found himself wrong about this too. After going through half a dozen lists of charitable organizations (Damn, there must be some serious money in other people's ills, he thought), he had settled on disabled homeless veterans as his charitable proxy, partly because of Makayla's struggling father, and partly because there were so many of them sprinkled throughout the five boroughs. It was a great use of the interns, but on Thanksgiving he had made a personal appearance – he had nothing else to do, anyway – and was able to turn the feast into a small promotional stunt for the upcoming show. While he had carved turkeys and served fixings, he had begun to take stock of the clientele. These were mostly old, mentally ill substance-abusing men who would rather drink or inject their meals. Initially Malcolm had felt pity and a sense of remorse: he had made his living off of more talented people while these men had sacrificed their healthy lives to preserve the system from which Malcolm and his cohorts greedily fed. That was a best case scenario. Most of them had given everything for absolutely nothing. Essentially, as he had deconstructed his professional life behind the counter, he had concluded that he was little more than a pimp. With these ruminations, Malcolm had been determined to make more appearances, *sans* cameras and reporters, to help these veterans-in-need. He had been honestly ready to make this commitment until one intransigent corporal had attacked him with a tray, accusing Malcolm of playing favorites with soup portions. The altercation had resulted in some nasty burns on Malcolm's neck and chest, and it quickly shook his resolve to be more generous.

The incident became a catalyst to Malcolm. He had spent many hours plotting and scrutinizing killing, but he had never physically harmed anything in his life. He was coaching Makayla on how to prepare her mind to fight against the social morals of taking another life, but he had no concrete experience to support his supportive speeches. He was learning, at least he assumed he was, how to become cold and indifferent to society's scruples and his own emotions. Taking a life for profit began to make more sense to him than simply exploiting that talent for profit. He slowly convinced himself that there was a certain honor in killing your own quarry after its use in life had dissipated. What was the alternative? he thought. Milking an artist for all he or she was worth and then letting them rot, like he had initially wanted to do with Nate? No, Brutus, there was no honor in that.

Unlike the animal that is slated for slaughter, celebrities and artists are completely aware of who they were when they were at the top. Their pictures, records, and films don't disappear, and most of these icons, in the minds of their fans, are never able to move past their most famous roles. Many fans, in fact, refuse to let their favorite stars change; through their wallets they demand that bands record the same album over and over again, until the group gets frustrated and tears itself apart. For the movie stars, audiences demand that each star stays forever entombed as the horror movie cliché, or the comic book inspired villain, or the western hero, or the child actor with overbearing parents. When these artists try to evolve, they become ignored. Those who can no longer draw in the masses are cast aside by their companies and labels. Eventually they end up hanging from rafters or lying in a pool of their own vomit like Nate Poulfry.

No, Malcolm would be doing his artists a favor by separating them from life while they were peaking. He began to believe these ideas, and he frequently repeated them aloud as he paced though his memorabilia room. He was becoming both physically (thank you, Mother Nature!) and emotionally isolated, and he was building the necessary strength and resolve to take from this world a human being.

On this particular evening, he was scheduled to transport at least six veterans from their respective homes to one of larger soup kitchens in Manhattan. He finally thought that the snow would work in his favor. He would use it for his first hunt and take one of these forgotten GI Joes as his first prey. A sudden twitch jerked through him and prompted him to grab his coat and make his way to retrieve the van from the parking garage. He made a point to let Charlie know he was heading for the kitchen and left.

The trip was slow-going. Malcolm stayed in the rough grooves, but constantly felt the wheel pull from his grip and spin in the opposite direction, as if something else were in control of his motions. He tested the acceleration by stomping on the gas and wasn't surprised with the spinning tires and the straining RPMs. He was getting a feel for how much control he had over the passenger van. It wasn't much. Without passengers, it was like driving a sheet metal sail. This would be perfect, he thought. He was willing to take some bumps and bruises – would have to unless he wanted to raise any suspicion – but he double checked to make sure this tin can at least had an airbag.

It took about an hour, but he made it to the first and only stop he would make that night. He double parked, got out into the cold, and lowered the ramp for the wheelchair-bound vet.

"Da fug take you so long?" the vet asked, clenching an unlit cigarette between his teeth.

"Bit of storm we've got going, sir. My name's Malcolm Spier, and I'll be your chauffeur tonight."

"'Scuses like assholes. Everyone's got one." (An old Army favorite.) "Name's Bill Sherton and I'm starvin', so if we can please get on with it, I'd appreciate it."

Malcolm trudged him off the snow-covered curb and onto the lift, jostling the poor man with every push and pull. He was trying to be as gentle as he could, but whoever had shoveled hadn't bothered to do so again in over an hour.

"My legs don't fuggin' work, but the rest of me can feel just fine, man. You wanna take her easy!" Bill bellowed through the howling wind.

"Almost there, sir," Malcolm replied kindly. Kindness and patience were emphasized in the brief training he'd received before working with the disabled.

Malcolm fumbled once more before getting the old man onto the ramp, and went down hard on a patch of ice. The old man chuckled as the lift ascended.

"Dumb-ass," he remarked.

Malcolm composed himself and secured the old man into the van. He locked Bill's wheelchair – well, almost locked it – into place, and jokingly told him to buckle up.

"Jus' drive the van, buddy," was the response he got.

The snow had ceased falling, but was being swirled through the streets and avenues by relentless drafts. Malcolm was taking it as fast as the storm and traffic would allow. While he was waiting at a red light, his phone buzzed and illuminated with a text. Malcolm swiped it off the passenger seat and read it intently. Thankfully it was in complete sentences. Someone older than eighteen was in charge of coordinating tonight, he thought. The message was clear and succinct: If you're already en route, come on down. If you haven't left yet, don't bother. We've already contacted the shelters to let them know that rides aren't coming. Drive safely if you are. God bless. Malcolm smiled. This was working out perfectly. Now where should…

"Light's green, numbnuts."

It sure was. Malcolm tossed his phone back onto the seat and gently pushed down on the gas. He turned on the radio to drown out any more of the asshole's observations. To Malcolm's amusement, Nate Poulfry and the Poulfries blared out of the speakers.

"Fuggin' love these guys," Malcolm heard from the back.

He smiled wider and quietly said, "Not half as much as I do, old timer."

Malcolm turned, signaled, and made a right to get off of the Long Island Expressway and head south. He wasn't going toward the tunnel anymore. The old man didn't seem to notice, or didn't care. Malcolm glanced into the rearview mirror and saw the man dozing from either a permanent high or a diabetic coma. He won't even feel it, Malcolm thought. He could feel his own pulse quickening. He rolled his perspiring hands back and forth over the steering wheel and began looking for a building, a large truck, or a wall that would win the physical standoff against his van. He wouldn't need much. The volunteer wagon was just a fresh paint job above being a certified pre-owned piece of shit. He rolled through a stop sign and found what he was looking for. There, just up ahead, at the entrance to St. John's was a snow-covered monument made of marble, granite, and bronze. Poulfry's song reached a crescendo, and Malcolm screamed in sync with Poulfry's moan and jerked the wheel hard to the left, careening across the double yellow. He put the speedometer's needle to twenty and figured that should be enough to do some minor damage. He hit the corner of the monument with the driver's side of the van.

A low, drawn-out groan brought him back to consciousness. He couldn't open his right eye, and he tasted blood in his mouth. He felt it seeping down his throat like a post nasal drip. He was bent over – actually the steering wheel and dashboard had twisted and curled onto him, and as he tried to free himself from his seatbelt, a tearing, wrenching pain ripped from his thigh to his neck and back again like a shockwave. He howled and cried and settled himself back into his unmoving position. He tilted his neck as far as the nerves would allow and looked down at his right leg. Blood was pooling at the top of his slacks, three or four inches above the knee. Uncontrollably, he vomited onto himself and cried harder.

"Owwuuuhugh…uuuphhhh," he heard from his right. He thought it sounded like air escaping from a punctured tire. He couldn't turn his neck to see, but the mangled body and wheelchair of Staff Sergeant William Sherton had finally given up its struggle with life. Malcolm thought he smelled smoke, but he no longer had the strength for reality. Before he passed out, he gulped down a shot of his own blood, whispered, "I did it," and vomited once more.

For a methodical man, Malcolm had seriously miscalculated the amount of damage that would be caused by a twenty-mile-an-hour collision. Five or ten would have been more than sufficient to dislodge Sherton from his chair and his life, but at least now there could be no denying that this had been a horrific accident caused by a worsening storm and an invisible, as its name implies, patch of black ice. Unfortunately for Malcolm, he would spend the better part of two months in traction with a severely fractured femur, a broken right wrist, a grade three concussion, multiple lacerations, two cracked ribs, and a ruptured spleen. Being nearly hypothermic by the time the paramedics arrived didn't help his chances either. The sound of the impact had alerted students in the Alfred B. Chester Dining Hall at the university, but instead of immediately calling the police, they had meandered to the scene and used their phones to record the carnage. It was posted on almost every social media site before anyone notified emergency services. One of the dining hall servers finally had the sense to call 911 and bring a fire extinguisher to put out the van's smoldering engine.

Charlie and Makayla met in the hospital lobby and went up to see Malcolm's unconscious seemingly mummified body. Both were shocked by his condition, but the doctor assured them that he was stable and that his coma was medically induced. They left flowers and cards from the staff and made their way to the cafeteria for some lunch. After each had taken a few bites from their sandwiches, Charlie began the conversation.

"That damn airbag didn't fire. I read the police report twice. I'm ready to go after GM and that damn soup kitchen," he said.

"How much could a soup kitchen be worth?"

"You honestly think they're serving up gourmet bisques and stews? If it's the water from a hot dog cart, I'd be amazed. Their rents are subsidized and most of their supplies are donated. They give a fraction of their collections to the food and veterans. Shit, most of it goes to pay salaries, very generous salaries at that. Don't be naïve, Kaylee, those are nothing more than legal rackets."

Makayla wasn't in the mood for any more educational

sessions, but she was mildly impressed that Charlie had come up with yet another abbreviation of her name. He had a different one almost every time they spoke. She couldn't care less who Charlie decided to sue, either. What she was most concerned about was the fact that her boss and mentor was completely useless with a little more than a month to go before the show. Pearle's health was steadily improving, and Makayla wasn't worried about The Oysters or Everett and his band, but Malcolm had kept his portion of the planning furtively hidden. She had found some notes on his desk and in his calendar, but she had no access to his computer or phone. When she had contacted the bands' agents, each had claimed that Malcolm had promised them an opening or closing slot in the lineup. She was almost sure that each was lying, but, knowing Malcolm, she couldn't be positive. Regardless of his lineup machinations, the show was going to go on, and it was coming up too soon. Charlie had assured her that he and his team had dealt with all the necessary legal aspects of the production. The TV networks and live streaming outfits were already setting up for the show, prepared and patiently waiting with their reporters, personalities, hosts, and cameras.

As if reading her mind, Charlie put down his water and said, "Try not to worry. The show is snowballing, and whether it's perfect or not is out of our control. Our captain is down for the moment, but his creation will live and rise and happen in just over four weeks. For now, let's enjoy the view of incoming ambulances, slipping patients, and these surprisingly decent club sandwiches."

They went up to see Malcolm before they left. They stood on either side of his bed like sentries, and Charlie spoke quietly, even though the room was private.

"Mel, they're eating it up with both forks. Jenna, the new girl in PR, spun the damn story all over the Web to make you a damn hero. You'd be shittin' yourself, buddy. *celebdirrt* has already done a small exposé with pictures from the crash site, and they called me earlier inquiring about some bedside photographs. They'll be up later on tonight. Cost me two hundred between the two security guards, but that's still dirt-cheap publicity. I'd never have guessed that anyone still gave two shits about record executives."

Out of his growing enthusiasm, Charlie began shaking Malcolm's raised casted arm, and several alarms blared. He hadn't realized that he'd made contact with his comatose boss, but these were exciting events. A nonplussed nurse came in and checked the monitors. The ululating shrieks stopped, and she kindly suggested that this might be a good time for them to leave. Makayla thought it was the perfect segue, and led the way to the elevator. She pressed the down arrow and folded her arms across her chest. She wouldn't speak until they were alone, and luckily not even a doctor was on board.

"That is too far," she chided. "He's barely alive, and you're arranging for some parasite to have a photo session with him?"

"Of him, Kay, not with him. They're not going to be selfies. Besides, Malcolm would love it. This entire situation is basically what he laid out in his office a few months ago. Shit, I wouldn't be surprised if it wasn't an accident. I've already selected the headline for the story, anyway."

"Who the hell do you know in publishing?" she asked incredulously.

The elevator stopped, its doors opened, and an orderly pushed in an unconscious middle-aged man on a stretcher. They both ceased talking and smiled at the worker.

"He going to make it?" asked Charlie.

"We're hoping so, but he is an organ donor, and we've got a good demand for those."

They had dropped two floors, and the orderly pushed the man out into the hallway and made a wide turn to the right. He left with a nod, and Makayla pushed the button to close the doors. She shuttered at the worker's cold demeanor, but figured it was one that had to be developed in his line of work. She looked back at Charlie and resumed her prior line of questioning.

"So, who do you know in the publishing business?"

Charlie waited for their floor before explaining himself. They exited the lobby, and when they hit the automatic doors, he began speaking.

"Back in the nineties, when there was still new music to produce, we had a few artists who thought people actually wanted to read their awful poetry and memoirs. I was always surprised at how well some of them could write lyrics but they couldn't string verses together to save their lives. Maybe it was their D-side stuff, I don't know. Well, Malcolm and I began a lopsided partnership, in our favor of course, with a local publisher called Dominion Books. We worked directly with one of their promotional guys, Aaron Milikin, for nine or ten books, I think. He also helped us out with magazine exposure when there was money in it. He was a very smart man. Must have been damn prescient, too, because when Web based publishing began, he jumped from his old ship and immediately bought into a start-up company. It ended up tanking in the early 2000s, but he still knew what he was doing, and he fell right into the lucrative world of entertainment publishing. Now he's one of the managing editors over at *celebdirrt.com*, and he called me more out of concern for Malcolm than for the chance at a story. When I told him that Malcolm would be fine, he asked me what happened, and I told him. After I told him, we started to negotiate."

Makayla didn't need the negotiations explained. What she did need was a drink and Alexis. She decided to catch a cab and take the train back into the city. Charlie had offered her a ride, but his house was fifteen minutes away from the hospital, and she didn't want to inconvenience him. She also didn't feel like talking with him anymore.

"I can stay with ya until your cab gets here," he offered.

"That's all right, Father," she said in a mock British accent.

He smiled and left her on the curb. What little light broke through the clouded sky was sinking on the horizon and she shivered. Thankfully, her cab spotted her, accelerated unnecessarily down the one-way path, and pulled up to the curb.

XVI

Malcolm's recovery was slow. His body was not in the physical shape it needed to be for an expedient recuperation. Before long the swelling in his brain subsided, and he was freed from the coma inducing medicine. He would have some lasting effects from the concussion, but his memory was astoundingly intact. He frequently cursed the brightly lit room, but the nurses patiently informed him that the lights were on their normal settings and that they had to remain that way for physical examinations. He also didn't like the grogginess that the painkillers induced, but he found the alternative to be much more unpleasant. What actually bothered him the most was the catheter. It had caused a mild infection, so after they took it out for treatment, it felt like he was pissing fire. That and defecating into a diaper had to be the most aggravating aspects of his recovery.

Weeks passed, and he was able to see the harsh winter storms begin to dissipate. As the weather got nicer, though, his flowers and get-well gifts began to wilt and disappear. At first he pretended not to mind. People are busy, he thought. They're busy because of me, he thought proudly. After a while, though, he felt lonely and in need of distractions. When he could focus without his head throbbing in excruciating pain, he turned on the flat screen and flipped through the channels. To his delight, he found a few lingering news stories about his crash and condition. When he saw the bedside pictures he did a double take, and then laughed.

"Charlie, you asshole."

Malcolm turned up the volume and listened to the newscaster.

"Again, the CEO of Spier Records and Entertainment is expected to make a full recovery, and their production of Pearle Collier and The Oysters' reunion show at Carnegie Hall has sold out. We here at JBC will be airing it live on TV and streaming it over the Web tomorrow night."

His jaw dropped as far as the bandages would allow. Tomorrow night? How damn long have I been here? he thought. Before he could answer his own question, the news continued.

"Finally, the associates at SR&E wanted us to remind you to keep the donations coming for their noble charity for disabled veterans, *Spier's for Spears*. It's a wonderful organization that transports our country's heroes from their homes or shelters to their healthcare appointments, jobs, meals, or rehab facilities free of charge. Contact information should be at the bottom of your screen. After the break, we will be live in Syria where the latest behea…"

Malcolm killed the TV and laughed again at the thought of it: if he knew Charlie, SR&E would be the sole proprietors of that entire non-profit by now. He picked up the bed's remote with his good hand and alerted the nurse.

"What can I do for you, Mr. Spier?" she asked.

"I have no idea what time it is right now, and you know what? I don't even care, but tomorrow night at eight I have to be awake. I've got to watch my show, and I don't want to be a damn vegetable through it. I need to be clear and lucid."

"Malcolm," she used his first name for bad news, "you're on a carefully controlled dosage schedule, and you need your rest." From the look on his bruised and battered face, she knew she was about to hear a wide array of curses and insults, so she quickly added, "I'll see what I can do about slightly adjusting tomorrow's dosages, but I won't promise you anything."

His composure switched from irritation and settled to one of victory.

"Thank you very much..." he glanced at the whiteboard to the left of the TV and saw her name "... Betty. I'm also thirsty as hell, and I need a changing."

Pearle Collier was as healthy as she was going to get. She had been drinking tea with honey and lemon and consuming gallons of chicken soup to combat her mild pneumonia, and she finally felt strong enough to take the stage. She had basically been speaking her way through the remaining rehearsals, and here she was, back in the venue that had helped catapult her to stardom, ready to fill the spotlight for one final performance, and ready to ignite the charge under her nephew's career. She wasn't rattled by the pressures; many other's careers had depended on her voice, and she had always done the best she could to bring them success and riches. She was endowed with a gift, and she firmly believed that gifts existed to be shared, not hoarded. The final sound check had happened a half-hour before, and she sat now in her intimate dressing room with Sylvan Thoreau. She sipped tea from a small porcelain mug and smiled at her former lover.

"Thirty years ago, we'da gotten my voice ready with something a little nastier than tea, honey," she said to him with a seductive wink and smile.

"You always were able to balance your filthy mind with a demure façade, my love," he said with a laugh. "I always had a blast warming you up before a show."

"It certainly helped me focus on something other than my nerves. If there were paramedics on site, I'd suggest we relive the past, but why tempt the fates? I think we'll both need something to look forward to for the post-show celebration, anyway. Are we about ready?"

Sylvan understood that the flirtations were over and that it was time to perform. He left the room momentarily to find the stage manager, and returned flushed and excited. He knocked lightly, but didn't wait for a response. Five minutes until the Poulfry tribute converted into the Pearle Collier extravaganza. As he closed the door, he stopped briefly to take her in, and all at once the years of lost love and opportunities overwhelmed him. He began to laugh at the joyous occasion that was unfolding and weep at his failed marriage and career.

"He sounds incredible." Pearle had been focused on the TV throughout Poulfry's tribute show, and she was referring to her handsome, talented nephew, Everett Beechum.

"You're on in five, my darling."

Pearle bowed her head for a few last minute prayers then made her way to The Oysters' dressing room. They awaited her arrival like soldiers anticipating the coming of their commanding officer.

"Let's do this once more, ladies. I love you all, and I couldn't be prouder to have worked with you."

They all joined hands and bowed their heads. After one…two…three…they made their way to the stage right marker and waited for the stage manager's instructions.

Malcolm wasn't sure how much of his ecstasy was drug induced and how much sincere, but he couldn't remember a time when he was as proud and pleased as he was at this moment. Collier's finale brought every gowned and tuxedoed person in the audience to a rousing standing ovation. After three minutes of continuous clapping and cheering, Pearle, her Oysters, and the band took their final bows, waved their final waves, and exited stage right.

"Ladies and gentlemen," the JBC host tried to say over the still thunderous cheers, "our post-show coverage will continue exclusively on the Web, so don't you dare miss a second. Coming up next at eleven is your local news. On behalf of JBC, Carnegie Hall, and Spier Records and Entertainment, I say goodnight, and I thank you for watching."

Malcolm turned off the TV and switched his attention to the tablet propped up on his food tray. He swiped the screen to bring it back to life and entered his password. He was immediately viewing the opulent lobby of Carnegie Hall. The cameras panned the crowd: a select group of fans and photographers who were flanking both sides of the small entranceway, awaiting the exit of the night's stars. When the doors finally pushed open, the sparkling Pearle Collier descended the small carpeted staircase. An uproarious applause began, and Pearle cupped her free hand over her mouth as laughter and victorious tears sprang from her eyes. Sylvan was by her side with his left arm locked around her right. The Oysters followed behind like a bridal party. The congregation waved and hugged and reveled in the celebration. Machine-gunning camera flashes bathed them, mainly Pearle, in bluish-white hues, and she swung her head to the left and right, allowing every man and woman get his or her shots. They cried out her name, trying to get her valuable attention.

Just as she was turning toward a camera near the lobby, when she was about halfway down the steps, a hysterical screaming erupted from the base of the stairs. Without warning, a man flew at Pearle Collier with the swiftness of a panther. All Malcolm and the viewing public were able to discern as he lunged at her was, "Etti, you bitch!" Before anyone could react to the attack, the man had Pearle's slender neck in a grip usually reserved for a baseball bat. The impact knocked Sylvan free from Pearle's arm and sent him careening over the bronze railing, also knocking The Oysters backwards like dominoes. Everett Beechum tried to get to his aunt from the top of the stairs, but tripped over Olivia Wallace's outstretched arm.

Makayla had immediately pursued her father, but she was not ready for his ferocity and speed, nor was she set up for a dash while wearing four inch stilettos and a strapless gown. The intertwined attacker and singer violently crashed into the iron spindles, producing a horrifying snap that reverberated through the silent room. The mass of dress and tuxedo tumbled down the final four stairs and landed on the red carpet runner with a thud. Alexis jabbed the syringe into Jordan's ass, but it was far too late. Pearle's chin lay at a grotesque angle from her chest, forcing her vacant eyes to stare toward the front entrance awning. Jordan Rogers, left lifeless by a massive stroke, slumped over Pearle's body in a perverted frozen image of senior citizens dry-humping.

The crowd's screams went silent as Malcolm's tablet fell from his good hand. It hit the cold sterile floor, splintering the screen into hundreds of shiny facets. It wasn't supposed to happen yet, he thought, and it sure as hell wasn't supposed to happen like that.

Part Three

Revising Vera Henlitty

XVII

"Jesus, Malcolm. How the hell do you think she'll take this?"

"Charlie, I don't really give a shit what she thinks or how she'll take it. She's lucky I didn't send her back to the glamorous world of baristahood. Her old prick of a father really screwed us with Collier. Couldn't have been worse timing. You know I could've convinced Sylvan to screw another show or two out of her. We were supposed to have at least another year of bilking her name and records, goddammit!"

"I'm not saying this won't work – based on what I've seen of these social media donation campaigns, we stand to make a fortune – but she knows a hell of a lot about you and this company, Mel, and if this rubs her the wrong way, she might start whistling to any reporter or cop who would be willing to listen."

"She won't. She can't. The only thing we could be remotely held responsible for Collier is not having enough security and any physical evidence left from Seitz has long been destroyed. We're clean."

"If that's the case, and if you plan on keeping ninety-eight percent of the donations, we should do just fine. What're you calling it again?

"I thought it up during physical therapy: 'Dash-for-Dementia'."

"And how are we supposed to make money off it?" Charlie asked curiously.

"It's simple, and it's pathetically easy to execute

from a production perspective. First, people video-tape themselves sprinting in front of those digital radars – you know, the ones in front of school zones? Next, they record whatever speed appears on the radar and donate that speed, in dollar amounts, to our veterans' organization. Minimum is ten bucks for the round, pudgy, slow bastards. Finally, they end their sprint with the phrase: 'That's my dash-for-dementia. I demand so-and-so sprint the next dash.' I've had interns sprinting all over the city," he added with a chuckle. "Oh, don't look at me like that. It exploits the morons who've mistaken the Internet for actual social experiences. These aren't the noble anonymous donors who fund the arts or medical research. These are the digital philanthropists who want their contributions to the betterment of society blatantly displayed for the web's approval. These people don't actually want to be near anyone who's suffering – in fact, they're probably guilty of walking around, or even over, a homeless drug-addicted soldier. It's practically a race to separate these idiots from their money, and this is one of the most efficient methods I've ever conceived."

Charlie looked at his smartphone and said, "Mel, this might actually work. Regardless of how you categorize our generous donors, we've been working for months now to redirect the public's attention away from the word murder and toward one that has a softer connotation: tragedy. Instead of Jordan Rogers being a nut-ball killer, he was the helpless, tragic victim of his own degenerative disease. This idea of yours should help calm the last remaining distraught fans."

"It's also going to help bolster the revenue shortage that Rogers cost us, so Makayla won't have a damn thing to say about it. That is why I didn't meditate over her possible moral objections."

Charlie sat across from Malcolm's desk, snuggly

secured in the leather love seat. He reached into his briefcase and retrieved the thick binder labeled in bold caps: PEARLE COLLIER. He turned it around and over to get it right-side up, and carefully fingered his way down the plastic tabs until he reached the one indicating *REVENUES*.

"Malcolm, it might not be as bad as you think. The people over at Musiikki have been contacting us for weeks, begging us to license and release Collier's full repertoire. It's the perfect time to sell it all because the prices aren't getting any higher. On the analog side of the world, her remastered and reissued albums are selling out faster than we can print them – buying that vinyl press was a great idea, by the way – and Ms. Henlitty's first draft of Collier's biography is being edited by the good people at Dominion Books as we speak. I doubt they would need to do much to it. Henlitty's a genius. How we were able to get that recluse to write again is beyond me, but she cranked out those pages like death stood behind her. If we can get the book published and released side-by-side with the Collier documentary, we could make anywhere from five to ten million by next summer. Those are rough estimates, but this could set us up for the best year we've ever had."

Malcolm contemplated Charlie's facts and figures in his bruised and battered brain. The epidermal swelling and discoloration had disappeared in the three months since Collier's show/murder, but the concussive repercussions and rather nasty scarring would remain with Malcolm for the remainder of his life. The plastic surgeon had expertly repaired what they could on the right side of his face, but the nerve damage to his once photogenic cheek was evident by a jagged lightning bolt of a scar. His missing teeth had been replaced with an orthodontic bridge, and his left leg housed more screws than most hardware stores.

He walked with a cane, an addition he actually found aesthetically pleasing, but physically exhausting.

His silence began to worry Charlie. Malcolm's new version of thinking was accompanied by a dead-eyed stare that resembled a high school sophomore sitting through a grammar lesson.

"Malcolm?" he inquired.

"I'm sorry, buddy. It still takes me a little while. I was just thinking everything over, and then I got to thinking about Vera Henlitty. I still can't believe she was willing to do this. She hasn't published anything in over fifty years, and all of a sudden she's cranking out a biography on an R&B singer! Has she ever published nonfiction?"

"Not that I know of. All I can remember from her is what my kids read in high school, *A Time to Weep*. It's been on school curricula for decades now. Apparently, though, she was quite a fan of Pearle Collier. Ed Tossle over at Dominion told me that Henlitty had a piecemeal manuscript on Collier's life lying around for years, and apparently the show and the tragedy were enough of a spark for her to contact her old publisher and make them a proposal."

"So what's our deal with Dominion?" asked Malcolm.

"We are splitting seventy percent evenly with the publisher. Henlitty's demanding and getting thirty because her name alone will send sales through the roof. She could've gotten much more, but she told them that she'd prefer to see the company outlive her. She's a very reasonable woman. What I was thinking, though, was proposing a generous sharing of our Pearle Collier documentary profits in return for sales of a newly printed version of *A Time to Weep*."

"And why would we care about a reprinted dated novel? Tell me that you've been planning and plotting a tragic mishap for Ms. Henlitty, dear boy," Malcolm said, paraphrasing one of his favorite Orwellian characters.

"The way I figure it, Malcolm, is the public believes in this dying in threes nonsense, so let's give them what they expect. Now wait, and just think about it for a second. Almost every school in the country would replace their raggedy copies with fresh ones after her death. Legions of fans would venture into their brick and mortar stores or onto their favorite online sites and buy newer copies – you said it yourself about separating these people from their money – and we could work directly with Dominion to produce yet another autobiographical/biopic venture."

"They own the rights to the film of *A Time to Weep*?" Malcolm asked doubtfully. "I didn't think that would ever be allowed to make the jump."

"They own the rights to pretty much everything, but Henlitty would only allow them to license the story for film production on the condition that they wait until after she's dead. I don't know, Malcolm. Ed tried to explain it to me last week, something about always wanting the novel to speak for itself and wanting to save and restore the literary tradition, or some bullshit. Don't try and rationalize authors' demands or behaviors, Malcolm, your head's in no condition to do it. What I do know is that it has the potential to make us a mountain of money."

"It certainly sounds perfect, Charlie. Let's adjourn for the moment, though. I've got PT in an hour, and I want to grab some lunch before the abuse."

Charlie packed his briefcase and asked Malcolm if he needed any help getting out of his office. Malcolm declined with a raised hand and a shake of his head, and Charlie left.

Before getting out of his chair, Malcolm checked his *SelfCenTierd* account to see how generous people really were toward their returning heroes. He smiled widely. In just over two days, they'd already raised 25,000 dollars.

Perhaps Jordan Rogers will make me more than Collier could have, he mused. He continued to scroll through and watch people's Dash videos, but was interrupted by an incoming phone call. Makayla's name flashed and faded across his screen several times before he answered.

"Malcolm?" she asked in a sobbing, stuttering voice.

"Jesus, Makayla. What's wrong? Catch your breath and speak," he said with genuine alarm.

"Malcolm, it's…it's my mother. She's…"

The cries coming from the other end of Malcolm's phone were hysterical. It sounded as if her phone had dropped. He leaned forward in his chair, thinking that the motion might somehow help the clarity of the connection.

"Makayla, are you still there? Hello! Ma…"

"She's dead, Malcolm. She had a heart attack yesterday climbing the Eiffel Tower."

His demeanor instantly shifted from paternally concerned to macabrely amused. He stifled a laugh, and said, "My God, Makayla. Whatever you need, let me know. We've got a ton of flier miles you can use, and I know the owner of the funeral parlor in my neighborhood. I'll ask him to help you get her body back to the States."

"I've booked the flight already, but I'm…" She cried and was unresponsive for half a minute. "I'm going to bury her in France. I don't care what it costs me, but I'm taking time off, Malcolm. I'm going to take a lot of time off. I'm sorry, but I was all she had left. Malcolm…"

And at this her end of the line went quiet, and Malcolm pressed *End*. He held the phone between his knees and stared through his open office door, into the hallway, through the wall, out toward the financial district, and…

He blinked and returned to his thoughts. Now who the hell is going to kill the author?

XVIII

"Gramma, what's the price on Dante's *Paradiso*?"

"Which translation is it, dear?" replied the store's namesake and matriarch.

"Arnest is the name at the bottom, Gram."

"Twenty-four, dear. Ask him why it's just the one."

Knowing full well that the elderly customer had clearly heard her grandmother, Alice Henlitty asked the question anyway.

"Not feeling like a trip through Hell or Purgatory on this beautiful summer day, sir?"

The wan man took his brown-bagged book and replied dryly, "I've been through Hell and Purgatory in my life, young lady. Not in Dante's proper order, but right now I'm looking for a bit of paradise."

The solemn customer looked once more toward Vera Henlitty, shambled to the exit, and left. When he was beyond the view of the bookstore's storefront window, Alice flipped up the hinged counter, followed his trail like a detective, and watched him walk up the road then turn out of sight. She hadn't seen him before, and this was too small a town to miss someone new. She had been indifferent toward the day to this point, but this odd, seemingly sad, and most-likely lonely man had piqued her interest. Sad wasn't the word, she thought. He was morose. She had been practicing her *SAT* vocabulary to please her tutor and mother, and that man was morose.

"Henny," she called, using her grandmother's playful nickname, "have you ever seen that guy before?"

"That was a gentleman, my dear, not a *guy*, and I haven't seen much of anything past three feet in front of me in twenty-odd years. So no, I cannot say I recognized that dude," she added with a smile.

She had been at least twenty-five years out of date in her slang, but she thought she'd try and amuse her favorite granddaughter. It worked as Alice cracked an embarrassed grin.

"It isn't polite to try and meddle in other people's lives, Ally, and I take it you thought he looked melancholy or lugubrious, no?"

Alice had been impressed with herself for remembering morose, but there went the all-knowing Oz.

"So you can see, huh, Gran? You've been lying to my mom and me," she knew better than to screw that order up in front of one of the country's greatest living authors, "this whole time?"

Vera raised herself from her cloth recliner and made her way down the slanted center aisle toward her granddaughter. The pace was slow and unassisted. Occasionally she'd reach out for a shelf, but she was still quite able bodied. Even though she was one of the most revered authors in the world, Vera Henlitty still worked the weekends in her family-owned bookstore. It was the only one in Ashua, and it was the perfect job for an author – a hack, she called herself – whose wish was to be left in peace. She had written three novels and dozens of short stories, but the only one people seemed to harp on about was her sixties classic, *A Time to Weep*. She had not been prepared for the publicity that the story had brought with it, so she decided to hide her family and herself in the cold, bleak state of New Hampshire. She had chosen the granite state in the late sixties because few in their right minds would stay longer than was necessary to fill up their tanks or grab a quick bite on their way to Vermont or Maine, and it was perfect in 2014 because barely anyone old enough to travel long distances bothered to read her work. If they had heard of a title, it was from some desperate tenth or eleventh grade English instructor, not from an internal desire to read a timeless coming-of-age story. The passing of years, in Vera's case, had finally succeeded in making her anonymous, and she couldn't have been happier. While she frequently chastised Alice's generation for not reading, she acknowledged to herself that the number of people taking pleasure from the written word was virtually the same now as it ever had been. It was yet another wasted American resource, as she had been begged by her publishers, family, and fans to begin writing again, but she refused to be the figurehead in the battle against the tidal waves of ignorance and complacency. The real reason she had resisted the literary calling was more private and closely-guarded than any secret she'd ever had: she didn't have any stories left in her mental vault.

Instead of writing, she had convinced herself and her dwindling group of close friends to take up small social causes. Over the years, her group became the subtle yet influential proponents of various feminist actions such as closing the substantial gap between women's and men's pay, access to inexpensive birth control, and paid maternity leave. At first, they maintained a strictly local presence by quietly picketing in front of the town hall or holding conferences at the local high school, but as the years progressed, technology and Vera's fame were able to propel their messages to a significantly broader audience. With the advent of social media, they could voice their opinions on myriad issues. They recorded videos and, although completely competent with their cameras and equipment, played up the fact that they were grandmothers who were attempting to use the newest technology. Their goofily inviting videos were incredibly successful in moving their opinions to the Internet masses because their tones were always light, the messages were never combative, and they refrained entirely from self-righteous demagoguery.

One particularly volatile topic, especially so in New Hampshire, and one that Vera took very personally, was the ostentatiousness of openly-carried firearms. Vera's second husband had been gunned down over a tragically idiotic traffic dispute, long before New Hampshirites voted to permit any of its citizens to bear their arms, and from that day, Vera decreed that human beings were too infantile and dimwitted to handle something as deadly as a gun. She and her group decided, after the Wild West free-for-all vote, that a powerful statement had to be made. For weeks they pondered how to counter the machismo of a blue-steel semi-automatic strapped to the hip, and they finally arrived at a deliciously lascivious idea. With the assistance of some of the younger members, the group decided that if so many people, men in particular, were hell-bent on brandishing their second peckers for the public to see, then women would brandish theirs too. So, after many blushes and giggles, the women went to their local box store, bought hip and shoulder holsters, and then returned to their respective homes to retrieve their personal massagers. They placed the plastic, glass, or rubber phalluses in their holsters and began wearing them around town, completing the day's errands as if nothing was out of place. They'd go out to dinner with them; they'd go to the movies with them; they'd go to the parks and the beaches with them. After many exasperated looks and a few minor confrontations, they recorded their plight and posted it on their newly created *SelfCenTierd* site. The campaign exploded across the county, then state, and finally the region. The absurdity of the dildo-wielding-grandmas, some with bandoleers full of erotic options, sparked precisely the reaction the ladies had sought: the open carry statute was amended to exclude public places and counties and townships that successfully petitioned to overturn it. Apparently exposing devices which bring pleasure was far more offensive than exposing devices which inflict pain. After months of openly carrying, Doris Filchik, the group's sergeant at arms, suggested they begin a buyback program but was quietly overruled.

Vera Henlitty at last made it down her bookstore's center aisle. When she reached her vibrant companion, she took a gentle hold of the girl's cleft chin and shook it playfully.

"There's quite a bit more to me than you'll ever know, my pretty," she said.

"There's a lot people don't know about you, Henny," Alice replied. "In fact, the most I know about you is that you're an incredible baker, a so-so driver, my favorite author, and, apparently, a quick judge of character. You are also writing again for the first time I can remember – I don't actually have any memories of you writing."

"Apparently my keen sense of observation didn't drown in the genetic pool. It's just a small project for someone who deserves better than the paltry attention she's now receiving. The media dolts seem to be focusing more on how she died rather than how she lived and what she contributed to the arts, and that is an abject travesty, my dear. That woman was to music as Austen was to the pen, and I will be proud to bestow the gift of her life's story to the generations…You should also know that it's time to close this dust heap and get home, and I'm driving."

The solemn, morose, melancholy, lugubrious man watched them from the rearview mirror of his rented car. The old woman and girl locked the front door of the quaint bookstore, got into their faded green VW bug, and drove away up the hill. There was no need for him to follow; he knew exactly where they lived. He bookmarked his copy of *Paradiso* and drove back to his bed and breakfast.

Malcolm scrolled through his contacts, but the names he sought were nowhere to be found; he must have purposely misplaced them when he switched carriers. He scrolled through the list once more and then opened his bottom right drawer. What emerged was the archaic Rolodex, only obsolete by fifteen years or so. He flipped the still rigid cards with his index finger until he came to his degenerate nephew: Spier, Walter. Wally's last known address was an apartment just outside of Manchester. It's been a few years, Malcolm thought, but how far could the bum have gotten? Walter was the youngest of Malcolm's late-sister's brood, and his chances in life had vanished immediately after his father failed to pull out in time. Walter never met this play-clock violator, and his mother did all she could to find another abusive, preferably drug-addicted, out-of-work partner. His childhood was pitifully Dickensian, and it produced exactly what the nation's premier psychologists predicted it would: a depressed substance-abusing individual with violent tendencies, sexual inadequacies, and anti-social behaviors. Malcolm had tried to help by taking the boy in over several summers and most holidays, but it had been too late to change the course of his life. Walter's sixteenth birthday summer, a humid one spent on Long Island with Malcolm, was the one that ended their relationship. Malcolm had overlooked most of his nephew's petty thievery, but he had to draw the line after Walter stole his Porsche and took it for an all-night joyride. Malcolm had loved that Porsche. Apparently he had loved it more than his own blood, because after letting Walter spend a day in jail, he sent him on the cheapest bus he could find back to his mother. As Walter grew older, his petty crimes morphed into felonies like drug trafficking, assault, and larceny. His relationship with his parole officer was the most stable one he'd ever had. Malcolm tried not to boast of his nephew too much when his family came up in conversation.

Malcolm's touchpad illuminated with the swipe of his finger, and he entered his security code. He brushed over the dial pad icon and tapped in the number. He raised the phone to his ear and heard a ring. That's a start, he thought.

"Uhllo?" said a semi-conscious voice.

"Walter?"

"An' may I asg who's callin'," the voice replied, gaining a bit more clarity.

Malcolm didn't recognize the voice.

"It's his uncle, Malcolm. Do I even have the right number? Hello? You still there?"

Malcolm heard the man on the other end clear his throat and empty his morning mucus into some unknown receptacle. What time is it anyway? he thought. He peaked up at the clock above his door that read 11:16. As he was getting lost in the clock's rhythmic movements, his earpiece came back to life.

"Well how the hell have you been, Uncle Malcolm? Ever get that Porsche runnin' again?"

Malcolm smiled, but wouldn't give him the satisfaction of hearing a laugh.

"Sure did, Wally. Spent what should have been your high school graduation money on it. Sold her a few years back, though. Made twice as much as I put in."

"I'm happy for you, Uncle Malcolm. I really am," Walter answered.

"Thank you, Walter. I'm surprised to have found you at this number. That's a good run for you. You finally turn your life around?"

"What do you want? It's been, what, five years since we last spoke? What do you need from me?"

"Walter, I never really gave a shit about the car, but what I couldn't figure out was why you turned your rage toward the one person who tried to do something decent for you."

"Is this really what you woke me up to talk about?"

Still a petulant asshole, Malcolm thought.

"It wasn't the point, Walter, but now that I've brought it up, how about a half-assed explanation?"

A long pause grew into an awkward one, but this one was not broken by a vulgar discharge of phlegm.

"How about we get to the damn point, Malcolm? I'm not exactly responsible for curing the ills of the world, but my job has me working nights, and I need to get back to sleep."

"You're more eloquent than I remember – prison's got a GED program?"

"Earned my Associate's while I was in for the last stint, now I'm going to hang up. It's been great talk…"

"I've got an extremely lucrative proposition for you, nephew. If you are interested, you'll stay on the damn phone, get some of the information, and meet me in two days at my Wissippee Lake house. You remember the address?"

A third silence began which Malcolm interpreted, incorrectly, as more defiance from his kin. It was in fact an honest misunderstanding of language. Walter had no clue what lucrative meant, and he needed several seconds to search for its definition. The prison program had only taken him so far.

"And how much are we talking, Uncle Mel?"

"That's more of a discussion to be had over some drinks and fish at the lake, kiddo," Malcolm responded. He added the term of endearment in order to tap into Walter's fragile psyche; a little nudge at the need for paternal attention could never hurt.

"I haven't been to that house since I was a kid. What about this weekend? I'm off for three days this schedule, so that would be better for me."

"This weekend will do nicely. I'll text the address as soon as I hang up. What's your cell number?"

They said a couple of perfunctory goodbyes, and Malcolm sent the address. The house had long been in disrepair; after he and his wife had stopped using it, he rented it for a few summers, but ended up letting it fall out of his focus. The roof had begun to leak, the paint to peel, and renters' inquiries had trickled and then stopped completely. It had been a decent passive income, but Malcolm only needed it now as a quiet place to negotiate some uncouth business. He picked up his office phone and dialed his secretary. (Thank you for that suggestion, Sylvan.)

"Emily, please cancel Saturday's Dash-for-Dementia press conference and my weekend PT appointments. Thank you very much."

Malcolm lurched from his chair, closed and locked his door, opened his personal safe, and carefully counted out ten stacks of rubber-banded 100 dollar bills. He took the stacks and placed them in a pocket of his gym bag. If he were lucky, this alone would be enough to encourage his desperate nephew; if not, the dashing morons would quickly resupply the coffers. He picked up his bag and cane and made his way out.

XIX

Vera Henlitty's neighbors were vehemently protective over her privacy. They treasured their author and were determined to have her as an Ashua resident for the remainder of her years. For decades her loyal followers fed false stories to unlicensed biographers and fame-seeking documentarians, presenting these out-of-town dreamers with faux-bumpkin mannerisms and outrageous histories until the credibility of their movies and stories was completely destroyed. These defensive tactics had proven to be extremely effective; after many years, the flow of leeching artists and authors had decreased – they had finally accepted that their fifteen minutes would have to come from a different carcass.

The good people of Ashua had gotten so efficient at warding off those interested in exploiting Vera that they were utterly confounded on how to handle someone she had personally invited. Her closest neighbors had to convene with her multiple times to discuss who would be in town and when. Vera was very amused with this fuss, and she happily played along. She dutifully informed them at one of their dinner parties that the first guest would be a man who had been intimately associated with Pearle Collier. His name was Sylvan Thoreau. No, she didn't have a picture, but they were quickly able to find his face on her granddaughter's laptop.

"My word," Vera said when she saw the online picture. "That's the gentleman who purchased *Paradiso*. He was in the shop not two days ago."

"Why didn't he introduce himself when he came in?" Alice asked.

"I have no idea, my dear. Perhaps I'm not the only one who doesn't enjoy attention from the outside."

"That doesn't sound normal, Vera," said Claire Dalimo.

"What do we really know about normal anymore, Claire?" Vera retorted. "Give John a call at the hotel to see if he's got a Sylvan Thoreau. If he's not there, we'll check Joanne's."

Sylvan had booked a week at Joanne's Bed and Breakfast and was enjoying his stay as much as he could. The devastation of Pearle's murder (he refused to address it as anything else) had left him emotionally distraught and physically shattered – the fall he had taken over the rail had ended with a fractured arm and bruised ribs. When he had recovered, physically anyway, he was determined to get as far away from the city and Malcolm Spier as possible. That man, someone Sylvan had once counted as a friend, was now devolving into something mercilessly avaricious. Only weeks after the incident, while Sylvan was convalescing in his midtown hotel, Malcolm had come to him with a generic get-well card and an idea about raising money for veterans through some ridiculous scheme involving people filming themselves sprinting. Malcolm had asked about Sylvan's health, but only in the most matter-of-fact way, and his offering of condolences for Pearle was limited to one very succinct sentence.

"It's time to look ahead, buddy, not backwards," the thing that inhabited his friend's body had said. "Of course it was terrible, but that doesn't mean that we have to give up all of the possibilities."

In a very deep recess of his brain, Sylvan began to believe that this new Malcolm was pleased with the awful turn of events. The Malcolm Spier he had known had never really been sentimental, but his response to Sylvan's grief had been eerily stoic. Sylvan had thanked Malcolm for his encouraging ideas, and then said that he'd need some time away. Malcolm had smiled, wished him a quick recovery, and left. As soon as he had been capable of doing so, Sylvan gathered his belongings and prepared for his trip home.

He had hardly been home for more than a month when he received a seemingly benign call from an elderly woman claiming to be one of his all-time favorite authors. At first he hadn't believed the aged voice on the other end of his phone, but gradually, as his mind narrowed down the possibilities of fraud, he concluded that it was in fact *the* Vera Henlitty, and she was interested in interviewing him extensively about his role in Pearle Collier's life. The polite Mrs. Henlitty, Sylvan finally learned, had volunteered to write the biography out of respect for an artist whom she had deeply respected.

Sylvan was hesitant to leave his home again, but he could not pass up the opportunity to meet the iconic writer. He had read *A Time to Weep* a dozen times at least, and always found new reasons to fall in love with it. He called back the number that Vera had left, and asked her a few more questions before he agreed to the interview.

"Mrs. Henlitty? Yes, hello. This is Sylvan Thoreau. I'm feeling a little better now, thank you. I just wanted to ask you some questions that I couldn't think of before. Yes, I suppose this does mean that I'm leaning toward yes. This shouldn't take too much of your time."

Sylvan and Vera had actually spent forty minutes conversing. He told her that he would slowly venture up to Ashua, but he hadn't given her any exact dates. She turned out to be incredibly genial and very easy to talk with, agreeing to his terms and wishing him a safe trip. While he hadn't realized it until he hung up the phone, the interview had already begun.

Vera had mentioned that Dominion Books was her publisher, and he had become viscerally suspicious. He had stood in front of his open fridge and let the chilled forced-air refresh his mind. It took several attempts before he had been able to get past the temporal image of the dead Pearle Collier, but he finally remembered why the name disturbed him: Dominion Books and the old Spier Records had once had a quiet partnership. Sylvan needed to know if Malcolm had any involvement with Vera Henlitty's newest project.

Malcolm sat in a rotten Adirondack chair and soaked in the warm summer sun. He looked out onto the pristine lake and took a sip of his bottled water. The day would be warm, but he hoped to be back on the road before the heat settled in. He looked at his watch; even though they had not agreed a specific time, he cursed his nephew. He picked up the tackle box and began to rifle through the assorted bobbers, ready to choose the winner when he heard the tires of a car crunching stones on the dirt driveway. A car door shut, and Malcolm gave a holler.

"In the back, Walter."

He didn't turn around to see the owner of the footsteps, but focused on impaling a fat squirming worm onto his hook.

"Uncle Malcolm."

At this he turned to see his nephew. Walter Spier had actually thinned out a bit. He wasn't what Malcolm would call desolate, but he no longer had the vitality of youth. He carried a six-pack of some dreadful lager and stood on the grass to Malcolm's right.

"Have a seat, Walter. It looks like a beautiful day for fishing."

"I can agree with that, Malcolm," Walter said as he

popped the top of a beer. "What the fuck happened to your face?"

"Don't drink too much, Walter. This is a business trip, remember? I was in a rather nasty car accident this past winter. Didn't catch the news?"

"Must have missed that story. Why the fuck is my generous uncle, after so many silent years, all of a sudden interested in my wellbeing? What the fuck can I possibly do for you?"

Malcolm baited the other hook before he replied.

"I know you've committed some serious crimes in your life, Walter, and I know that many of those were responses to the horrific shit that was done to you. I need to know something else."

"And what is that?"

"I need to know what value you put on human life, Walter. I need to know if you have developed scruples."

"Scruples?"

"Morals, Walter. Were you ever able to learn right from wrong?"

"What I've learned?" Walter leaned forward, trying to look intimidating. "Uncle, what I've learned is what I've needed to do to…"

Malcolm didn't feel like continuing this line of conversation any longer. He turned to look his nephew in the eye.

"How much would it take for you to kill?"

Walter sat back, embraced his uncle's stare, and imbibed a contemplative gulp of warm beer.

"With the money you must have, Uncle, why the hell are you asking me this? You telling me that murderers are hard to come by in New York?"

"If I'm going to spend the money it takes to get something like this done, I figured I'd extend it to someone I know needs it."

Walter absorbed this and ran his finger along the can's sharp curved opening. "It depends on who it is, and where it is. For family, I think I might do it for twenty thousand and a damn secure place to hide out."

"I can give you ten right now, and all you'd have to do is perform a robbery-gone-wrong. There's a sweet old lady in a town called Ashua, and she owes me money. I would like you to collect it for me."

"An old woman, Malcolm? You want a gramma dead?" Walter asked with a laugh.

"And anyone else who happens to be with her, yes. Twenty thousand plus whatever's in the place, and then I will provide you with a very secure hideout in the Arizona desert. It's remote and almost completely off the grid."

Malcolm cast his baited hook and watched the ripples rise and fall, rise and fall. Not a bad toss, he thought. Walter opened another beer and watched his uncle. He finished half the can before he spoke.

"If I'd had to bet on how this conversation was going to go, Malcolm, I would have lost every dime. I've got a job, even if I fuckin' hate it, and my life is about as steady as it's ever going to get. I'm not exactly clean, but I've been a free man for a long time now, and I'm almost beginning to like it. Almost."

He finished the can and let his thoughts settle into the oncoming buzz. He picked up the rod Malcolm had set aside and threw out his line. They fished silently for several minutes before Walter broke it by cracking another beer. He pulled the brim of his hat low over his eyes and talked to his knees.

"I'll tell you what. Make it thirty-five, and I'll shake your hand right now. "

Malcolm reeled in a few clicks and smiled at his nephew's shrewdness.

"Like I said, I've got ten with me now. It's in the

bag next to the tackle box. Take it. I can get you the rest by next weekend, and you can stay here until then. The power's back on, and it still keeps most of the weather out. In fact, why don't you get some work done on the place while you wait? It'll be a decent cover story if anyone comes by to ask. Are you at all handy?"

"I picked a few things up over the years. I can patch the roof where it needs it, hang a couple of new doors, and take care of some of the siding."

"The place needs it. I'll stock her with food before I leave. If there's anything else you'd like to find in the house, anything that the store won't sell, tell me now."

Walter hesitated briefly before timidly responding, "Tweak."

"What the fuck is tweak, nephew? I'm in the business of producing records not keeping up with the latest drug slang."

"It's meth."

"Don't think that's big around my parts. Tell you what, why don't you take what you need out of the duffle bag? Take care of what needs taking care of, and meet me back here at seven for dinner."

Walter reeled in his empty hook, took several bills out of a stack from the bag, and left without a goodbye. Malcolm's line began to dance and gyrate with tension, and he arched the rod toward his body.

"Would you like me to continue?"

"For a little longer, Mr. Thoreau. I'm sorry for the delays, but I seem to fade along with the sunsets these days. Please hit the record button for me."

Sylvan had been recounting his life, love, and times with Pearle Collier for three days and three evenings, and he too was both physically and mentally fatigued. He had just finished recounting his divorce from Pearle when Vera asked him for a respite and some coffee. He brewed a small pot for them both and took some time to poke around the store again. When he had purchased his copy of Dante, he had been performing his half-assed version of reconnaissance. While he had no doubts about Vera Henlitty's motives, he had many misgivings about who was funding and profiting from her project. He needed to be sure that Vera was truly independent in this venture, free from any influence or pressure from Dominion Books or SR&E. He also needed to be sure that Malcolm Spier and his young protégé, the one whose deranged father had murdered Pearle, were nowhere near Ashua, New Hampshire. He had promised himself that he would leave without even a word to his literary hero if he detected anything related to his former friend. To accomplish this, he had tried to remain covert when he'd come to town, but he was no man-in-black and Henlitty's network of neighborly nans had tracked him down to Joanne's Bed and Breakfast within a day.

The coffee maker beeped shrilly. He moved toward the rear of the office and poured a small cup for Vera and a larger one for himself, then sat back down at the dinette table. The back office of the bookstore was little more than a walk-in closet, but the ceiling fan helped circulate the cool, dry evening air.

"Would you like any milk or cream or sugar, Mrs. Henlitty?"

"Black is fine for now, Sylvan, and would you please call me Vera?"

"Would you have called Pearle by her first name?"

"If she told me to, I would have."

Sylvan laughed because he knew that Pearle Collier would have insisted, and she would have been insulted if Vera had refused.

"All right, Vera. Let me finish half of this mug and I'll be ready."

"See. Isn't that more comfortable?" she said with a wink.

He drank down two mouthfuls of steaming Arabica coffee, wiped his lips on a paper napkin, and began to speak.

"When we split and went our separ..."

His speech was cut off by the sharp jingling of the front door's bell.

"I'm sorry, dear. Alice must have forgotten to lock the door at the end of her shift. Let me go and send them on their way, and we'll finish up for the night."

She hit stop on her recorder and went to get up, but Sylvan raised his hand and got out of his chair.

"I can manage to tell a lost tourist that the store's closed. I'll be right back."

She nodded in appreciation and leaned back into her rocker. He pulled the door toward himself, and the office light cascaded down the center aisle of the store. Its energy faded just feet in front of the door, and in that gap between the seen and the unseen, Sylvan made out a lanky silhouette and the tips of two very worn and filthy work boots. Had it gotten that dark, that quick? he thought.

"I'm sorry, sir, but we're closed for the evening. Try again tomorrow at eleven and you might even get a chance to meet Vera Henlitty in the flesh."

"I need some books," said the stranger.

Sylvan started down the aisle and politely repeated his line, leaving out the part about Vera. There had been no reason in Sylvan's mind to act defensively, so his hands remained loose at his sides. He could not have seen the framing hammer that the stranger concealed behind his right leg. When Sylvan was finally able to register the pale, drawn stubbled face that had been hidden by the darkness, he realized that this man was not here as a patron of the literary arts. Before Sylvan could react, his temple and

130

forehead were caved in by a terrible upswing of the steel hammer. His body, while not yet lifeless, crashed against the shelves of the Young Adult display and then rolled limply to the carpeted floor. He would die before the arrival of the EMS team.

The stranger took a moment to survey his first victim and then continued up the ramp to the office. Two brief, strident shrieks were all the eloquent Vera Henlitty would manage before she was brutally murdered.

Malcolm was reading a newly printed copy of *A Time to Weep* when he heard the driveway gravel give way under Walter's skidding tires. He placed his bookmark on page 106, threw the book onto the floor next to the overturned coffee table, and reached down the right side of his recliner. The room was in complete disarray, and that was only partly due to Walter's renovations. He had tweaked and worked steadily through the nights and days, leaving each new project unfinished.

The rear door opened, and Malcolm heard his nephew make his way through the kitchen. He came into the light. Malcolm sat forward and flinched when he saw the splatters of blood that painted Walter's arms, torso, face, and hat brim.

"Uncle Malcolm…it's done," Walter declared and moved into the living room.

He raised his right arm, took off his hat, and began to rub his bloody face into his bicep. When his nephew's eyes were momentarily covered, Malcolm quietly drew up the twelve-gauge that he had earlier stationed next to the chair. He pushed down on the barrel, using the weapon as his cane, leaned forward, roughly aimed at Walter's torso, and fired. Walter's body fell backwards, not like a body from an action movie that flies five or six feet, but more like a boxer going down after taking a tremendous hook.

Malcolm moved away from the creaking chair, took his phone out of his pocket, and dialed 911. As it rang, he built up his hysteria and shrieked into the mouthpiece when he heard the line "911, what is your emergency?"

"I just shot my nephew! I think I just killed my nephew! I shot him! Send an ambulance!"

"Sir, please stop screaming. Please calm down, and tell me where you are."

"Oh my God! Oh God!"

"Sir, please, what is your address?"

"Oh my God...eleven Eas...we're at eleven East Drive, Wissippee Lake. He was attacking me! He had a hammer!"

"Are you hurt, sir? Are you sure your nephew is deceased?"

"No, I'm not hurt, and he's not moving! He came at me with a hammer!"

"All right, sir, officers and an ambulance are en route."

"Oh my God. Oh my God," Malcolm said as he slipped his thumb over the end button.

He put the phone in his pocket and walked over to Walter's corpse. The buckshot had ripped through his skin, muscles, lungs, liver, stomach, and heart. The close range had prevented the pellets from spreading out and had resulted in a guaranteed kill shot.

"Walter. This is the most generous thing you've ever done."

Blood began to pool and seep into the wood and carpet as the sirens approached. Malcolm fell back into character when he heard the officers' commands.

"We're in the living room. My nephew needs help!" he shouted.

The controlled chaos that is a crime scene investigation ensued.

*

"So you had no idea your nephew was working on all these projects in your house while he was high on crystal meth?" asked Detective Wortens.

"I wasn't at the house while he was doing most of the work. Like I said, I wasn't planning on getting the place ready to rent until next season, maybe for deer season if he worked quickly. I was trying to let him work at his own pace."

"And you trusted him to stay and work with all that cash and your belongings lying around?"

"He swore that he'd been clean for months, and he's family. I've always had a spot in my heart for him. I was paying him in increments of cash through the summer. I thought it would keep him honest. I thought that…" Malcolm paused and rubbed tears from his eyes for a sincere effect.

"He had been doing good work, and when I spoke with him on the phone, he sounded energetic and mostly lucid. I guess what I interpreted as exhaustion might have been the effects of the drugs. I just…I just never thought he'd attack me."

"When he arrived home, you said he was covered in blood and wielding his hammer?" the detective continued.

"He entered through the back door, and slowly came through the kitchen. He stood in the living room entranceway, splattered in blood, and told me that if I didn't give him the rest of his money right then he would bash my skull in and take it. I stayed in my chair, trying to keep the situation calm, and then he drew the hammer out from under his shirt. It was covered in blood, and it looked like something else, maybe hair, was stuck in between the claw. I asked him whose blood was on him, and he stared at me. I repeated the question, and he took one step toward me. He couldn't keep still. He was twitching. He took his hat off with his left hand and brought his right arm up so he could rub his face."

"That's when you shot him?"

"He had taken down my gun rack to paint, and my twelve gauge was near the armrest of my recliner. I know it's not the safest thing to do, but I keep them loaded. I don't have any kids, and I haven't rented the place in years. I...I..."

Malcolm folded his arms on the table and bent his sobs into them. Detective Calvin Wortens finished his notes and offered his condolences to Malcolm. Before leaving, he brought his suspect a fresh cup of water. This was a horrific incident, but it appeared to be a rather clear instance of self-defense. In his investigation, Wortens had discovered that Walter Spier had a long, lurid criminal history. He had been arrested on four occasions for possessing and distributing crystal meth, and he had also become a user of the drug. Wortens had found out that this useless sack of shit was responsible for savagely killing Ashua's beloved Vera Henlitty and a man named Sylvan Thoreau in an apparent robbery gone wrong. Personally, Wortens had hated Henlitty's book (he'd been one of the millions forced to read it in high school), but he was horrified at how Walter Spier had killed them. Although Henlitty's bookstore had landmark status, Wortens couldn't think of anyone who would want to inhabit that building again. No, this seemed to Calvin Wortens to be a horrific tragedy that had ended with a degree of righteous justice.

While Officer Wortens had not understood the depth, complexity, or beauty of Henlitty's writing, millions of others around the world had. Individually and collectively, they wailed and mourned, lit candles and read passages from her stories, and spoke of her death as if it severed the last tenuous tether which held a generation of Americans to the dying pastime of reading. Professors, teachers, and self-appointed scholars unanimously proclaimed that the world would never again see an author of Henlitty's wit, style, or talents. Who would now be capable of transcribing the angst of the youth or capturing the zeitgeist of our constantly-evolving world?

Part Four

Remastering Spier Records & Entertainment

XX

Late summer always irritated Malcolm. Its heat and humidity were oppressive, and the explosion of vampiric insects made his yard intolerable at any time of day. He thought back to his childhood and could never remember the mosquitos being out in the hottest parts of the days, but in the last few years a new breed of flying leeches had made its way across oceans and settled in the beautiful suburbs of Long Island, NY. He wasn't annoyed with the heat or the insects at the moment, though; he was actually quite comfortable in his climate controlled memorabilia room. Three displays were complete, and the fourth was in the middle stages of construction. Three signed copies of Henlitty's most famous works, sealed tightly in a small glass case, were surrounded with some of the author's quotes, letters, pictures, and fan-testimonials. Above them was her headshot, the same one as used on the back cover of *A Time to Weep*, signed and acknowledged by the deceased author to the good people at Dominion Books.

The outpouring of grief, from both the mass markets and esoteric literary circles, was massive. Neither Malcolm nor Charlie had correctly estimated the value of Henlitty's life and influence, and Malcolm was immensely satisfied when he rejected Ed Tossle's request to renegotiate the deal they had made for reissuing Henlitty's most treasured novel. No school system would order music albums in bulk, but thousands of them, both private and public, had ordered hundreds of new copies only days after her horrific murder. Many districts also ordered the scripts for the stage production, a medium in which he allowed Tossle complete control (no need to make enemies at this point), and as of late August, Vera Henlitty's catalog of works had brought in more revenue than both Poulfry and Collier together. Malcolm was just finishing his copy of *Weep*, a book coated in a dried mist of his nephew's blood. Now, however, he didn't have the time or patience for a close analysis. He was expecting company. Makayla and Charlie would be at his door at any moment, and he needed something to drink.

As he opened the fridge and extracted an ice-cold summer ale, Makayla rang his doorbell and Charlie knocked to the rhythm of Nate Poulfry's famous hit, *Bricks and Mortar*. Malcolm smiled and answered the door.

"Nice touch, Charlie. Come in and leave your shoes on. No point in trying to keep it clean," he said. "Makayla, how are you?"

He immediately read betrayal and anger in her countenance, but he would not address those emotions at the moment. Instead he embraced her with an all-in-one welcoming/consoling hug which she did not reciprocate with any trace of affection. She had spent most of her time away in Europe, France in particular, where she and Alexis had dutifully followed the route that Etta Rogers had specified in her diary. They had been in Pairs when Makayla saw the Dash-for-Dementia promotion on her phone. She had nearly fainted, but was brought back to consciousness by Alexis's quick reaction and her own personal rage. How the hell could Malcolm have exploited her father like that? How the hell could he have posted Jordan Rogers's pictures all over that damn website while she was across an ocean burying her mother? For Makayla, this was too far; she was beginning to suspect that Malcolm Spier was capable of far more heinous schemes. As her disgust of her boss percolated, she also experienced a fleeting remorseful thought of the role she had played in exploiting the lives and works of Nate Poulfry, Seitz, and Pearle Collier.

Her brain had worked seamlessly to convince itself that those situations were different, and therefore acceptable. Those people – those clients, rather – had greedily sought out SR&E to rekindle their personal fames and fortunes, but her father had been a helpless, pitifully tragic victim who had committed a horrific act. He had served his country and had returned as a decorated soldier who led the best life he could, a life that had been ended by a debilitating disease. She had decided on the flight home that she couldn't continue working for someone like Malcolm Spier, couldn't keep following the methods of a psychopath, but she would disguise her intentions behind her best poker face and wait for the most opportune time to make her exit from the company.

Malcolm released Makayla from the hug and shook Charlie's hand.

"Something to drink?" he asked them both.

"Beer would be great," Charlie said.

"Just some ice water for me," said Makayla.

He provided the beverages and led them to the memorabilia room. They sat down on the museum-like benches, and Malcolm began immediately with the point of their visit.

"Charlie, please explain this situation again. Makayla, are you aware of this at all?"

"Only with what Charlie told me on the drive over."

"Do you remember the tiny town where Poulfry died?" Charlie asked.

"Cristol Springs?"

"Impressive memory. Yeah, well that little shithole of a hamlet has a mayor and a chamber of commerce who are in the process of producing their own Nate Poulfry tribute festival. It's scheduled for Halloween weekend. They're in a bit of a jam because we own everything related to Poulfry – everything but the songs he covered, that is. So this mayor, Andrew Lamprey, called me the other day requesting our permission to use his songs for the show. I offered him a partnership and our expertise instead, but he refused, so I quoted him a price for the songs. He eventually told me to shove it up my ass. Not very couth for an elected official, but he then informed me that the show would be produced with or without our permission. He went on and on about Poulfry being Cristol Springs's native son, so I thanked him for the courtesy-call and hung up the phone."

Charlie took an inch of beer out of the pint glass before he continued.

"Malcolm, we could sue them if they use the material, but it would cost us and it might murder our image. Naturally the courts would side with us, but it would take months, maybe years, to resolve. I was busy working out the options when the good mayor called me back and proposed a more personal meeting with our legal team and Poulfry's representatives out in the beautiful Colorado town of Cristol Springs. He apologized for his brusqueness in the earlier call and demanded that we start over. He also insisted that we come to see the proposed site and the festival attractions, but I told him that any decision like this would have to be made by you, Malcolm."

Malcolm scanned the section of his room dedicated to Nate Poulfry and spoke.

"I think we'll be able to convince the good hicks of Cristol Springs that a healthy partnership can be quite beneficial. I'm assuming you've already arranged our terms, Charlie?"

"A rough outline, yes. We get seventy-five percent of

the ticket sales and thirty percent of the vendors' takes. If they don't like it, their audiences will have to enjoy two days of the few songs Poulfry covered."

"Why don't we let them have the damn festival?" Makayla interjected. "Let's just license them his greatest hits, collect our share, and call it a success."

Malcolm and Charlie looked at her, honestly dumbfounded.

"This is our material," Malcolm affirmed. "And how can we record more dementia dashers if we're not the official co-sponsors of the show?"

Makayla's face broke at the comment. She excused herself and went to the bathroom. Charlie squirmed like a teenager asking for a first date, and Malcolm turned his attention back to his old friend.

"When did the good Mr. Lamprey say we could come?"

Charlie composed himself after a brief pause, and said, "He suggested the Friday after Labor Day weekend. He listed some flights that go directly into Colorado Springs Airport, but I told him we could make arrangements with a private charter. I do have a friend whose son flies private jets. Give me the word, and I'll book the plane."

"Book the flight now," Malcolm said with a smile. "We'll make a damn nice weekend of it."

Across the country, in the Rocky Mountain region of the Midwest, Detective Ray Delijo crouched in the shrubs in the pre-dawn darkness. He and a small squad of narcotics officers had suddenly halted and were trying to meld themselves like chameleons into the foliage of the forest. The point man had triggered the domino-like drop and was now silently indicating the night vision camera which hung ominously from a Ponderosa Pine. Its Sauronic lens pointed toward the northwest trail while the hunting party approached stealthily from the south. They'd had to make their way in that direction, but now they would have to take an even wider-arced detour. They kept low and moved in a staggered formation toward the target.

Colorado's decision to legalize marijuana was a momentous boon for its citizenry and its tax coffers, but a poisonous thorn for its illicit suppliers. Since their customers were now buying marijuana from clean, safe storefronts, the devious entrepreneurs had increased their production of meth and molly, and had started pushing their merchandise with increasing violence, mercilessly defending their dwindling territories like cornered animals. They had found a new clientele in the influx of out-of-state natural gas workers, and the Regional Commanders of all four districts had had enough. They had coordinated with the local FBI and DEA offices to root out and destroy the serpentine syndicates, not so much for the safety of the public (although that was what was espoused at news conferences), but for the threat of cutting into the enormous new tax profits. Politicians were discovering that the supply side of drugs was much more lucrative than the seek-and-destroy tactics of old; they, like the Mexican cartels and the Colombians before them, had figured out that being the only show in town made the most fiduciary sense. Both the donkeys and the elephants were building careers off their highly taxed marijuana, and they would be damned if they'd let groups of two wheeled dirtbags ruin their burgeoning political futures.

One man in particular, Mr. Andrew Lamprey, mayor of the small town of Cristol Springs, had his aspiration meter set very high. Two years prior, he had brought the weed industry to a reluctant chamber of commerce, and the jeers quickly turned into extolments when the town's revenues broke records for two consecutive terms. Lamprey did not consider himself to be a corrupt politician – no more so than your average elected official – but he knew that if he were to build his reputation and grow his career, he'd need a massive amount of money, and he despised fundraising. He would not do anything that would be obviously illegal; rumors spread quicker over the Web than a bacterial outbreak in a hospital, so he had to figure out a subtler plan. He found what he needed in the mourning fans of Nate Poulfry. A tribute festival. Of course, he had thought. He and the C.o.C. would produce a tribute festival for Colorado's most celebrated musician, and Lamprey would grant limited selling permits to vendors of all kinds, charging them exorbitant fees for the privilege of selling to the thousands of stoned Poulfrites. Lamprey would then establish separate accounts for the permit fees. He would take a small percentage from each deposit to amass his political fortune. It would have been a simple, easily-executable plan had his legal team not mentioned a company named Spier Records and Entertainment. They owned every legal right and license to Poulfry's material, and without their approval, no one would play his songs. Lamprey's modest dreams of holding a meaningless job with a fancy title were instantly obliterated. For the first time in his life, he had wished for term limits, but the job of Cristol Springs mayor didn't exactly bring corruptible powers or chances of fame, so the people never thought it necessary to impose limits on an incumbent. Unless he recused himself from office, he had the job for as long as he desired. Unfortunately, he needed the position to stay relevant in Colorado's political sphere, and this company from New York was about to fuck up his perfect little dream.

Lamprey had spent weeks thinking about ways to produce and host the Poulfry Tribute Festival, but every idea was met with resistance from his legal team. He needed the rights to the music, and his town really didn't have the money to fight a drawn-out court battle, so he decided to look for some type of leverage against the label. He read through the articles pertaining to Poulfry's accidental death, looking for something that he could link to SRE, and his meticulous studies had finally paid off. He would need some assistance in corroborating what he'd figured out, and as fate would have it, drugs would come to benefit his career yet again.

"That's perfect," he'd said aloud to an empty office. "That's absolutely perfect."

XXI

Ray Delijo didn't mind his new assignment in the least. Crime and Cristol Springs had never been synonymous, and he was getting very tired of investigating minor infractions, domestic assault cases, and, still, Nate Poulfry's overdose. It had been close to two years since the singer/songwriter had expired, yet the honorable Mayor Andrew Lamprey was hounding Delijo's lieutenant for the answers he wanted to hear. Lamprey wanted someone to be held responsible for a tragically unfortunate accidental death. Delijo did not look forward to picking up that file later in the week, but for now he let the adrenaline and cool morning air carry him toward the hopefully occupied cookhouse.

While the raid failed to produce any human quarry, Delijo and his team were successful in confiscating many pounds of both ingredients and finished products. Prior to obliterating the makeshift lab with probably more explosives than were necessary, the group had gathered what intelligence they could, along with hundreds of pictures, and were satisfied that their superiors would have something to parade to the press. Dawn had broken, but the air would not release its chill. On the way back, the team abandoned its crouching posture, but was still very careful. These suppliers had taken to booby trapping their areas with a plethora of surprises, and fortunately the trip home was safe and uneventful.

Delijo returned to his station to shower and change and then he would go home for a good day's sleep. His wife would be at work, the house would be quiet, and he would draw the drapes and soundly sleep in his memory-material mattress. After he'd showered, he felt his pockets for his phone, but it wasn't in any of the usual spots. He cursed because now he'd have to swing by his desk, which meant he could get snagged into someone else's bullshit. He grabbed his gym bag, kept his eyes on the floor, and made his way out.

Luckily, his phone was in the top-right drawer of his desk, and better still it had been off, so the fickle battery would still be somewhat charged. After several moments of letting it find its network, he noticed the symbol for a new voicemail. He lightly pressed the screen and listened.

"Detective Delijo," an unfamiliar voice said. "This is Sergeant Offlund of the Boulder Police Department. If you would please give me a call immediately at 303-555-3839, I'd appreciate it. We've arrested your son on some rather serious distributing charges, so please call me back as soon as possible. Again, it's 303-555-3839."

"Dammit, Javier," he said as the message stopped.

For Ray Delijo, rectifying this situation called for something slightly more inventive than letting his son endure the consequences of his actions. To keep his boy as a free member of society, he would have to reach out to someone who had slightly stronger connections than his lieutenant. Without any other options, however, he threw his phone into his bag and sprinted up the stairs to his superior's office. He attempted to maintain his forward momentum, turn the door knob, and begin explaining the severity of the situation all in one motion, but his shoulder struck the door's frosted glass first, followed by his head. The impact sent glass flooding into the office of a seated, bewildered, and marginally hung-over Lieutenant Deborah Philips. She watched as one of her best detectives struggled to right himself through her destroyed door. There was some blood, but he looked to be more embarrassed than physically harmed.

"I will take cream and sugar, if that's what you needed to know," she said sarcastically.

Delijo composed himself, carefully opened what was left of the door, and spoke urgently.

"My son's been arrested up at his school, and I need your help. The Boulder boys have had him locked up since last night, and I don't know how the hell I'm going to fix this."

Philips stared at him, her mind beginning to work through the favors that were owed to her, the people she could contact for help. She plucked her pen from its brass plated holder and wrote two phone numbers onto her legal pad. She tore the sheet on its perforations, folded it, and passed it across her desk.

"I'm going to call beforehand to explain who you are and why you'd have those numbers. Wait a half-hour and dial the first one, and if no one answers that one dial the second. Before you head out, clean up the cut."

"Thank you. I'll let you know what happens, and I'll have my paperwork for last night ASAP."

He left the precinct without tending to his head. The blood dried and his hair matted, but he'd take care of that later on. He called his wife at the first stoplight, and she seemed to be much more composed than he had been. She calmly told him that she'd call their lawyer. Delijo then explained where she should send him. He wanted to use Philips's contact, whoever it was, but his boy needed immediate legal representation. Ray Delijo was an intensely private man, and he wanted to keep the business of his family from the ears of his always whispering neighbors.

He spent as much time glancing at the digital clock in his car as he did watching the road disappearing under his front tires. His home was roughly forty-five minutes from his job, and he decided to stop at a diner parking lot to make his calls. He parked diagonally from the front entrance, plugged his phone into the jack, and dialed the first number on the folded yellow paper. It rang four times, and just before the voicemail sequence commenced, an enthusiastic voice answered.

"Detective! Let's chat."

Delijo recognized the voice but couldn't place it.

"I'm sorry to bother…" he began, but was cut off.

"Detective, please. Let's get to the point," the voice said, descending into a solemn tone. "An old friend and confidante of mine told me that your boy is in quite a bit of trouble up in Boulder. Now I've got some very good friends working with the DA up there, former college buddies ironically enough, who would be delighted to help out."

"He's not an evil kid. He's no damn saint, but if he was dealing anything, he wasn't out to hurt anybody. Shit, he probably wasn't even out to make money. He's always been lonely, and he probably thought that the assholes he sold to would be his friends."

"We'll figure all of that out pretty soon, detective. Like I said, my connections are sound. What might be challenging, though, is what you're going to have to do for me."

Why can't I place this voice? thought Delijo. It sounds like a commercial announcer trying to sell hope and promise and America and…he finally had it.

"I will do whatever it takes, Mayor Lamprey."

"Excellent. And you've got a sharp ear. What I need from you, Detective Delijo, is to finally find something, anything, that incriminates Malcolm Spier and his company, SR&E in the death of Nate Poulfry."

"Mayor, I…"

"Delijo, I'm going to have to get very creative in helping your boy, so I expect you to use every imaginative investigative technique in your repertoire to find me something that will help me put together my Poulfry Tribute Festival. You see, the bastards own every damn note Poulfry ever wrote, and without the music, we'll have no show. With no show, we'll have no revenues, and with no revenues, we'll have no…You can see where I'm going with this, can't you? I need you to look closely into what types of drugs killed our man, and then I want you to find out where those pills came from. If you can't find their exact source, I want you to start making calls to any physicians who have worked with that company. If everything turns out to be Kosher with them, I want you to get creative with the facts. I want you to continue this investigation as soon as I hang up the phone. Are we clear?"

"I'll turn around right now and begin as soon as we hang up."

Ray Delijo made a call to his wife. He promised that he'd meet her and Javier in Boulder as soon as he could, but right now he had to get back to the precinct. She vehemently protested, but he calmed her down and explained what his returning to work would do for their son.

When he got to his desk, he found Poulfry's file on top. Attached was a note from Philips that read: *Lamprey told me to dig this out for you. If you need any help, let me know.* He opened the manila folder and flipped through the reports, diagrams, and photos until he came to the copy of the coroner's report. He read the same words that he had already registered hundreds of times before, but now he began to think closely about the prescription pills that had speckled the rock star's floor. He could have picked them up in Cristol, but it wasn't likely. Delijo and his former partner had interviewed all of the usual peddlers, but most had given up the illicit life to work for the legitimate distributors. He also went to the handful of pharmacies and private practices, but each had all of their supplies accounted for. Whatever Poulfry had on him had come in with him.

Delijo's thoughts then traced a new line. There had been a nurse with them. Her name? He flipped back to the witness testimonials and found Alexis Drison. He thought very carefully about the pattern he was creating. He wasn't thinking in terms of justice or the law; he was thinking about getting Lamprey the answers he wanted so his son would have a second chance at living freely. He created the assumption that Ms. Drison, an employee of Spier Records and Entertainment, could be arrested and charged as a suspect in Poulfry's death. It was a damn stretch, but all Lamprey seemed to want was leverage, not a solid foundation for a legal battle, and this would be a perfect piece for his negotiations. Delijo continued to read the report and invent the connections he needed. He switched on his computer and began typing.

It was near lunch when he finished the addendum to his old report. He hit redial on his phone and made his second call to the generous Mayor.

"Well, my fine sleuth, that is the best news I've heard all morning. That is so damn beautiful that I'd like you to help me personally deliver it to the CEO of Spier Records and Entertainment and his representatives. They will all be here at the end of the week."

"Anyway I can help, Mr. Lamprey. I'll email my report now. Have you heard anything from your connections in Boulder?"

"Don't worry, Ray. According to the ADA, many of the witnesses have less than stellar records, and not one of them seems to be able to remember what they allegedly bought from your son. Javier, that's his name, right? He will probably spend today and tonight in their lockup, but he seems to be holding up. The bail will be low, even lower now, and you will have him with you by tomorrow afternoon."

Delijo exhaled an exhausted yet relieved breath. He rubbed the bridge of his nose and pinched his eyes shut.

"I can't thank you enough, Mr. Lamprey," he said when he finally regained some energy. "If there's anything else I can do..."

"Why, there is, in fact," Lamprey said, cutting off the detective. "As I said, I've invited those soulless parasites to an informal conference in our beautiful town, and I want you as my contact. We are going to take Malcolm Spier and his people on a picturesque tour of our less frequented sites."

Raymond Delijo agreed without questions or protestations. This man, irrespective of his reasons, had helped to keep Javier free. After agreeing to a brief meeting, Delijo ended the call, grabbed a coffee and a sandwich, and prepped his mind for the two hour drive to Boulder.

XXII

Malcolm's residual injuries were not agreeing with the hiking that Mayor Lamprey had scheduled for the day. His right thigh, with all its hardware, ached miserably, he was short of breath, and no matter how much water he drank, he was suffering from a merciless thirst. While the late summer heat was dry, a point that had been repeated by almost every native he had encountered, he was still uncomfortable and irritable. When he had agreed to fly to Colorado for this meeting, he had envisioned eviscerating this hick-town mayor in a brief one-sided boardroom duel, not trudging through the wilderness like the goddamned Donner party. The terrain was uneven and rocky (living up to its moniker), and his straight-out-of-the-box hiking boots were not providing the grip that he needed. He was supposed to be SR&E's general, but out in the wilds of nature he could barely maintain the twenty-foot gap between himself and the rest of the troupe. Even his own people were letting him fall behind without so much as a glance backwards.

Both Makayla and Charlie had been instantly smitten with Mayor Andrew Lamprey's relaxed, confident charm, his athletic swagger, and the sincere love he professed for his state and all its natural beauty. He had made them feel immediately at ease by personally picking them up from the airport – well, his friend and liaison to the local police department had driven – then taking them to lunch in a quaint bistro at the base of Taskins Peak, and finally (what Malcolm was detesting at the present moment) leading them on a guided hike around the foothills of the mountain. If his supposedly loyal employees had bought the smile and the 'your-home-is-my-home' routine, Malcolm thought, he had not trained them well enough.

"You doing all right back there, Mr. Spier?" Lamprey shouted.

The question shocked Malcolm out of his internal miseries, but he refused to show his agony.

"Just making sure we're leaving only footprints," he responded.

"This is just the warm-up. Tomorrow we're taking you deeper into the beautiful wilderness of El Paso County," Lamprey added enthusiastically.

"Can't wait."

Makayla relished in Malcolm's obvious misery. She could have sworn that Charlie was getting some pleasure from it too, but he was nearly impossible to read. When Andrew Lamprey had turned to check up on Spier, she watched her boss tremble in those ridiculous boots. He was in obvious pain, and even in the arid air his sweat was visibly profuse. He proclaimed that moving forward would be an excellent idea, but his body language begged them to return to the sanctuary of the hotel. Lamprey seemed to have understood Malcolm's discomfort, but he would not let the novice outdoorsman leave the crisp fresh air after such a short trek.

Makayla was enjoying the day, but she also felt like getting back to hotel. Alexis had flown out with the rest of the group, but not as a part of the business team. Malcolm, who had once been somewhat generous, had demanded that if significant others were flying on the company's chartered jet they would have to pay, so Makayla had forked out the lofty fee, feeling even more resentment against her former mentor. Charlie, however, had pulled her aside and assured her that the plane's rates didn't break down by the number of asses in the seats, so she wouldn't have to open her wallet at all. Charlie was frequently becoming the reserved balance to Malcolm's strange behaviors.

In the present moment, Alexis was probably shopping in the little town or visiting the site of Nate Poulfry's final concert. While she was completely level-headed in her professional settings, she was also quite sentimental, and she had mentioned visiting Poulfry's climactic concert amphitheater before their flight had lifted off the ground.

Although Alexis had not been on Lamprey's original guest list or adventure-filled weekend itinerary, he and his associate, Detective Ray Delijo, seemed to know exactly who she was. The detective had reminded the ladies that he had been in charge of Poulfry's grisly crime scene. Both of the women had thought it odd that the detective still referred to the hotel room as a crime scene, but they quickly forgot about the point when Lamprey started reciting the history of the town and surrounding area viewed through the windows of the van.

Only Andrew Lamprey and Raymond Delijo were privy to the real reason for this rather intense opening stroll. Hiking them before they'd had a chance to acclimatize was a tactic that Lamprey had decided to use to disorient and exhaust his east coast opponents. When weariness and discomfort had overtaken their focus and resolve, Lamprey would dictate the new terms of the Poulfry Tribute Festival negotiations. The good mayor was hoping that two straight days of mountaineering in the thin Colorado air would break Malcolm Spier of whatever obstinate business mindset he had. Delijo was hoping his new partner's tactic worked quite a bit quicker and one afternoon of abuse would suffice. He still had a son to move home and a family to stabilize.

If the walking and climbing and lumbering didn't

work, Lamprey and Delijo would then present Malcolm and his team with the evidence they had creatively uncovered. They would confront the drained group with the proof that Poulfry's unnecessary prescription pills had been illegally obtained by his then nurse, Alexis Drison, through Spier's private physician, Isaac Baylin. Of course, Lamprey and Delijo had not searched thoroughly enough to prove any of these circumstantial theories, but they were inadvertently correct. If they'd had the patience to do so, they would have been easily able to prosecute Malcolm Spier and his company for the death of Nate Poulfry, but Cristol Springs's newest power couple wasn't really intent on solving a mystery.

So far, the exhaustion tactic was working splendidly. Spier looked like he was a step or two away from a coronary, and the others, while much more polite and amiable than their boss, were not exactly at their athletic peaks. Lamprey and Delijo would walk them over the stony path and under the strikingly blue sky for another half-mile before turning them back to the cars. Lamprey earnestly hoped that the business end of the discussions would remain professional; as much as he proclaimed to court and overcome confrontations, he secretly detested them. He'd never rehearsed a good-cop, bad-cop routine, and he really didn't want to have his initial audition during this weekend excursion.

Lamprey halted the party for some water and gorp and explained that, after a little while longer, they would head back to the car. He promised that after a nice dinner at the hotel's restaurant, he would finally let them get some rest. Charlie and Makayla were still attempting to maintain their appreciative and enthusiastic guises, but Malcolm's had all but evaporated with his back-sweat. Delijo took quick notice of Spier's sulking and tried to be helpful.

"Don't worry, Mr. Spier. Tomorrow we'll be covering a whole lot of this ground in a pair of UTVs."

Malcolm stared at the detective while chewing some raisins, peanuts, and granola. He attempted to look threatening and imposing like a seated mafia don, waiting another moment before he spoke.

"The fuck is a UTV?"

"It's like a golf cart on steroids," Delijo responded, unfazed by Malcolm's pathetic attempt at intimidation, "and it will help prevent any serious medical conditions associated with obesity."

Malcolm looked down at his gut and back up to the detective, who was now chewing his own handful of granola and confidently grinning. Delijo stood from his rock, took a swig of water, and walked away.

"Let's get moving, people," Lamprey proclaimed. "We've got some very sacred ground to cover before we turn around."

When Lamprey began babbling about the strength and majesty of the Comanches, Malcolm feigned an extreme pain in his leg and fell over. He coated the performance in screams of agony and implored his guides to cut the trip short. The mayor and the detective reluctantly agreed, and they made their way back to the van.

"You think that bald prick will try and dodge tomorrow's trip?" Lamprey asked Delijo.

"I think his partners, or whatever the hell they are, will convince him to go. You heard them at dinner. They sounded embarrassed that they had to stop today because of him, and I think they'll make sure he's up and ready in the morning."

"I think you're right, but the man's a damn shyster. Hopefully after tomorrow we'll never have to see him again. This location of yours has been completely secured?

There are no surprises waiting to dismember us civilians? I've heard about the sick shit those backwoods chemists do to protect their stashes."

"We scoured that area for hours, destroyed or dismantled anything we found, and left it a smoldering pile of ash. It's secure, and it will have the exact effect you asked for. If the site itself doesn't persuade them, we'll hit them with the drug/manslaughter angle and let them mull it over. Either way, we'll get what we want."

Delijo finished his reassuring speech just as he pulled up to the mayor's home. Lamprey wished him a restful night, asked quickly about Javier, and then left the detective alone in the van. Delijo hesitated before he put the van in drive. He was thinking about what he had left to say to his son. He had kept him free from the horrors of incarceration, but had failed in accepting Javier back into his home as the boy his wife had delivered into the world. Ray Delijo, the son of two hard-working immigrants, had never been on this side of an extortion deal, and he was not enjoying himself. The more Lamprey asked of him, the more Ray resented his son. He was too proud to be anyone's puppet, and as soon as this was finished he and Javier would have a very serious discussion about their new roles as father and son. As he pulled into his own driveway, he thought about how his wife would respond to this conversation. He figured she'd resist, and to counter her maternal reaction, he'd employ every interrogation technique he knew to convince her that there had to be serious consequences to this detonated bomb of a situation.

He carefully closed the van door, waved hello to number two-fifty, and went inside his house. He was happy to find his wife asleep on the couch and his son reading in the den. He paused in the doorway and took stock of his only child, shook his head, turned, and went upstairs. He would lay down the new rules tomorrow, after this business with Lamprey and SR&E was finished. Delijo showered, brushed his teeth, and went to bed. Exhausted, he fell into a deep, restful sleep.

"My goddamn leg is killing me, I can't catch my breath, there isn't enough water in this fucking state – hand me that glass – to quench my thirst, and we're supposed to go on another fucking nature walk tomorrow? Is this how business is run in this part of the fucking country? Dammit, Charlie, what the hell are we doing here?"

Malcolm's question was strictly rhetorical. He didn't care about any answer Charlie would offer, he just wanted his second in command to know that this supposedly simple excursion was a complete failure. Charlie wasn't appreciative about being belittled by a boss for whom he had been funneling the burgeoning Dash-for-Dementia funds into several new fictitious nonprofits organizations. If they were discovered by the proper authorities, they would land them both in jail for what could very well be the rest of their lives.

And while Malcolm hadn't said much to anyone about Vera Henlitty's horrific murder, Charlie had not needed a connect-the-dots painting to figure out what had really happened in New Hampshire. Although he himself had been the one to mention the benefits if the writer happened to disappear, he never thought Malcolm would take a personal role in her execution. The poor woman was in her nineties, and nature would have surely done its work more gracefully and respectfully than Malcolm had done his. Her frail, once comely face had been bludgeoned beyond the point of recognition. Her skull had been caved in as if caught in a compactor. The police had actually found some shards of her skull partially driven into the floor of the office. Malcolm had unleashed this primal rage, yet had returned to New York as the victim. He had returned believing his own bullshit story. After Malcolm had settled back into the office and routine, Charlie realized that his once sacrosanct role as his friend and confidant had been permanently erased. Malcolm had unofficially demoted him to the equivalent of one of the nameless and faceless employees. Charlie, a man who had only ever known loyalty and comradery to the Spier family, had been discarded like a Henlitty novel in a student's locker. Initially, he refused to believe that his friend would do such a thing, so he had made the extra effort to try and be genial with Malcolm, but nothing seemed to work.

"You have any suggestions, Chuck, or do I have to ask you again?" Malcolm said impatiently, interrupting Charlie's thoughts.

"We'll all go out tomorrow to appease the mayor, to try and kill him with kindness, if you will, and if he doesn't start talking business by tomorrow evening, we'll get on our plane and take his festival dreams with us. The worst we can come out with is some great exercise and fresh air."

"You have anything to add to that genius, Makayla?"

"For someone who has absolutely nothing to lose and only a ton of money to gain, you really show your appreciation beautifully, Malcolm. As far as I can make out, based on the numbers Charlie drew up, we can afford to hike a few trails and license out a few of Poulfry's songs."

Malcolm finished another glass of water and silently walked to the bathroom. He swung the door partially closed and left piss in, on, and around the bowl. He reentered the suite and looked at the two people he had up until recently considered his closest allies. He didn't exactly know what to think of them now; he was too damn drained at the moment to figure out what to do with them either.

"Get me in the morning so we can get this shit over with," he said, signaling the end of the team meeting.

"If you can tell me of a place that has more beautiful, more awe-inspiring, perfectly pristine and symmetrical natural wonders than the glorious state of Colorado, please tell me now so I can book the flight," Mayor Lamprey posited in his best tour guide voice. .

Malcolm was trying to keep his right leg extended yet stable as the UTV bounced through the increasingly dense undergrowth of the diminishing trail. The front passenger wheel struck a concealed rock and jostled the unsecured record executive into the molded-plastic canopy of the vehicle. He had scoffed at Lamprey's suggestion of latching the seatbelt, and now he cursed as he fell toward the seat at the perfect angle to crush his testicles between his thighs. He grimaced at the initial burst of pain and dreaded the rush of nausea and discomfort that would last for the duration of the ride.

"I'm guessin' that jolt took your mind off the leg, huh?" Lamprey jeered.

Malcolm tried to respond, but could only get out a low expletive and some spittle.

"How...how much...farther?" he managed to ask through the throbbing pain.

"Probably a half-hour or so depending on traffic," Lamprey responded, laughing at his own joke.

Delijo, Charlie, and Makayla followed behind the mayor and Spier, keeping a safe separation of twenty yards or so, and Charlie braced himself as the vehicle barreled toward the camouflaged rock. Unlike Lamprey, Delijo maneuvered, as carefully as the terrain would allow, around the coffin-size slab of mossy gneiss. Charlie took notice and sent an appreciative nod toward his cautious chauffeur. Delijo extended two fingers from his curled hand and quickly glanced to the back seat.

"Comfy back there, Ms. Rogers?" he asked, still astutely focused on the trail.

She hollered back what sounded like a yes, and he put a bit more pressure on the accelerator. Lamprey was beginning to put some distance between them, probably trying to jar Malcolm out of the remaining bits of his bullshit arrogance, Delijo thought, but going too quickly was legitimately dangerous on these paths. To begin with, they were purposely left overgrown by their druggist proprietors to prevent outdoorsmen from venturing too close to their cook houses; in addition, they were barely wide enough for the smallest of all-terrain vehicles, so one slight mistake would leave them stranded in a very remote and brutal part of the forest; finally, while the authorities, including Delijo, had cleared these paths as best they could, they were bound to have missed some of the more nefarious booby traps. There simply wasn't enough light in the mountain-day to clear each and every one properly, and these operators were crafty and deadly when protecting their merchandise. Ray decided that they were going fast enough, so he grabbed at his walkie talkie and spoke.

"We do the best we can clearing these paths, sir, but we don't always find all of their surprises."

Lamprey didn't respond, but Delijo knew that his new friend had understood the message when both brake lights lit up. Delijo let off his own gas pedal. The deceleration allowed conversation again, and Charlie took advantage of the opportunity.

"Not to sound ungrateful for the grand tour or the hospitality and history lessons, but what the hell are we doing out here, detective?"

"We're almost there, and you'll appreciate the journey when you see the destination," Ray replied. "If you haven't guessed already, we're slightly unorthodox out here – one of the few states that'll vote consistently red, focus on other people's families, yet set up drive-through weed dispensaries...I wouldn't trade it for anything."

"I think it's great," Makayla interjected from the back. "I think it's damn enlightening."

"Actually, I agree with you, Makayla, but this is something that could have been taken care of in a couple of hours in your boss's office, Ray," Charlie added.

He realized that the detective either didn't know or wasn't at liberty to divulge the reasons for all the traveling, but just as he was about to try a different line of questioning, he saw the trail widen into a small clearing. It was no larger than a little league infield, and as far as Charlie could tell there was nothing impressive or significant about the site. He saw Lamprey's crookedly parked vehicle, its two occupants removing themselves from its confines. Lamprey seemed to spring back into form, while Malcolm braced himself against a tree and creaked and cracked into shape. Delijo parked to the right of the lead vehicle and, reminded his passengers to take all of their belongings before exiting the four-wheeler. Charlie and Makayla moved toward Malcolm while the detective walked the perimeter of the clearing. His posture contradicted the levity that he had exuded on the drive up; he seemed sincerely concerned that some danger had been overlooked in his prior investigation. He seemed to be searching for some lurking beast, one that was ready to maul this unsuspecting group of politicians and business folk.

Lamprey seemed unperturbed about his friend's agitation, and offered his canteen to his guests. Malcolm took it first and finished most of it. The mayor wouldn't let his contempt of this man show yet, but he was truly beginning to dislike Malcolm Spier. He was also beginning to understand that Spier's obstinate nature might lead them to a nasty confrontation. Yes the man seemed fatigued and disoriented, but the two days' worth of excursions had failed to temper his anger. In fact, it seemed to bloat with every new step they took, and, to Lamprey's chagrin, Malcolm did not seem to be any more willing to engage in polite negotiations for the rights to Poulfry's music. Malcolm Spier, like a bloody and beaten brawler, seemed to be reserving the last vestiges of his strength and wits for some unspecified final round.

"Hope you brought something a little stronger than water for this trip, mayor," Malcolm said after he had finished the remnants in the canteen.

"I would not advise drinking anything stronger than a sports' drink out here. We're going to be heading up some steep, touchy terrain in a little while, and you really have to stay focused."

"I think my team and I will manage just fine."

Malcolm hobbled away from the mayor and joined Makayla and Charlie at the south-east section of the clearing. The pain in his groin had finally ceased, but with each step he realized how raw his feet were. Another day in these boots would almost certainly lead to a double amputation at the ankles, so he decided to try and expedite this deal by not taking one more step than was absolutely necessary. He grumbled his miseries to his two employees. They both thought it was poor form not to see this journey to its end, but, in a typically subordinate fashion, both acquiesced to his will.

"Hey, Mr. Mayor!" Malcolm exclaimed. "Whadda you say we cut the Boy Scout shit and get down to business?"

"It's only a little farther up that trail," Lamprey said,

motioning to an area that looked like only trees and bushes to the New Yorkers. "This little patch isn't proper enough for what we have to discuss, anyway," he finished.

"I'm a patient man, Lamprey, but I am also sharp enough to know when I have an advantage, and in this particular fucking instance, I'm holding all of the best cards. Unless you're planning on putting a gun to my head, we're not taking another damn step."

Lamprey ignored Spier's taunt and beckoned Delijo to retrieve the crude landscaping tool from his UTV. Delijo ceased his perimeter search and went to the vehicle's surprisingly expansive trunk, unhinged its clasp, and extracted what looked like an oft used machete. He made a point of slowly unsheathing the blade, letting it scrape against its case like a samurai's sword. He turned it over, inspecting the edge, allowing the bright midmorning light to reflect into Spier's eyes. When the faux inspection was finished, he let the blade drop to his side and walked quickly toward Malcolm, Makayla, and Charlie. Malcolm ever so slightly flinched as if to run, but settled his nerves when the detective politely asked him to move out of the way – the path that needed clearing was directly behind Makayla. As soon as he reached the brush, which Makayla saw was actually less dense than the rest of the circle, he began cleaving a patch about three feet wide.

"We cleared this area a few months back, but nature's already reclaiming it. Seems to suggest that no one's been back, or it could mean that they've found a new trail to their old spot," he said between hacks, addressing no one in particular.

Spier swallowed and asked, "Who would be dumb enough to come back to a spoiled spot?"

Delijo ignored the question and replied, "These assholes use others."

"Pardon?" Malcolm asked.

"They traffic in workers from South America or Mexico and put them to work in these labs. They herd them like livestock, preying on the desperate, and threaten and torture them into compliance." He paused from his work and continued, "They drag them out here, force them to live next to their fields or trailer-labs, and work them day and night. They're shown how to cook or cultivate, and then left to their own devices. Whatever group is in charge will supply them with weeks worth of canned goods, and after a couple of months, the finished product better be ready."

"Why don't they run?" Makayla asked, horrified at what she was hearing.

"The area is booby trapped by whatever narco gang is in charge. The surprises aren't only meant for outside intruders – they don't bother telling their slaves where the traps are set, and they don't mind if they lose a few here or there. The work continues until we arrest them or they're killed. Whenever one of those two things happens, the gangs move on to their other sites, but we're beginning to understand that they use a twisted sort of area-rotation cycle. They know that we don't have the man-power to monitor all of the sites at once, so we do our best to destroy everything we find. Like I said before, these people are vicious parasites who use others to expand their own riches and power. I don't care if I'm always a step behind, I want them to pay for the pain they inflict on innocent, hard-working people."

Malcolm seemed almost envious of the cartels' efficiency, but Makayla and Charlie, whose demeanors had drastically shifted from mildly interested to devoutly attentive, were genuinely beginning to reflect on the career paths they had chosen.

Charlie, more so than Makayla, knew that these

infrequent moments of self-contemplation were always fleeting – even after nearly seventy years to practice – so he decided to try to extend this instant by looking carefully at whom he was with. He first looked at the beautiful young woman who stood in front of him. True, she looked like the last couple of years had aged her at least five, but she was nonetheless very pleasing to the eyes.

He then looked to her left and saw Malcolm. Like a tourist, Malcolm was trying to get a signal for his phone. He was poking it up in the air and then swinging it in exaggerated arcs as if that would help. Charlie looked away just before Malcolm's eyes would have met his own. When this is over, Charlie thought, I'm done. I'm going to retire and get as far away from that prick as possible. Before he could plan out his entire end-of-work strategy, though, Andrew Lamprey moved up on Malcolm's right and firmly encouraged them all to move forward to the path that Delijo had cleared.

"Believe me," he said, "you don't want to be late for this lunch."

Malcolm shrugged the mayor's hand off his shoulder and waited for him to walk out of earshot.

"Let's get this shit over with, and just for the record, old buddy, we're doubling the price we were going to offer him. If he doesn't like it he can fall off this fucking mountain."

"I'll take the lead, Malcolm. Wouldn't want you tripping over any leftover wires or falling into any holes," Makayla said impatiently.

Malcolm looked at her like a father who's received his first taste of sass from his perfectly mannered honor-roll achieving daughter. She didn't wait for a response; she too wanted this ordeal over with, but not for the same reasons that Malcolm did. Similarly to Charlie, she thought that this would be the last transaction she'd partake in with

Malcolm Spier and his company. She had gained enough experience to work for a legitimate label at this point, and Alexis could find a job in any state she wanted. Makayla was no longer afraid of the consequences of leaving Malcolm and his warped ideas behind, but she would repent for ever having thought him a wise man later on in her life. Now, though, she needed to separate herself from his influence for good.

The final part of the journey culminated at what looked to be a manmade plateau carved into the side of the mountain. It was, for the most part, level, and the ground underfoot was comprised of dead pine needles layered upon rock. They had reached it only after a fairly steep hike, and it was a respite that everyone seemed thankful for. Lamprey and Delijo moved closer to what looked like a small cave near the mountain and returned with a couple of logs.

"We making a fire?" Malcolm inquired.

"With these?" Lamprey asked incredulously. "Much too thick for firewood. No, you and I, and whoever else wants to sit for a while can use these as chairs. Not the most comfortable, but they will suffice. There are more of them right inside that cave if you're interested."

"Why, again, did we have to hike up to this lovely piece of real estate?" Malcolm facetiously asked.

"As the detective alluded to back at the clearing, this is an area that was recently used by some very awful people. These people…"

"Sell drugs. Yes, I heard your *DARE* lecture half an hour ago, so I'll ask again with less decorum: why the fuck did you bring us here?"

Lamprey's final bits of patience and propriety were now gone. He turned to Delijo, and nodded.

"And now he wants to do this the messy way. May I please have the newest Poulfry file, detective?"

"What does Nate fucking Poulfry have to do with this?" Malcolm barked in an explosion of aggravation.

Lamprey held the large manila envelope in his hands and brought himself back to his calm center before attempting to speak to Malcolm.

"In the great state of Colorado, especially here in El Paso County, we will not tolerate the carnage, pain, or suffering brought on by illegal drugs. You and your company are little more than pushers in fancier clothes," he said as he broke the seal of the envelope and removed the papers. "Nate Poulfry's official cause of death was determined to be a coronary failure brought on by an overdose of prescription pain pills, *Triazalep* to be precise, and for the longest time we could not figure out where he'd got a drug like that. It's not common at all in Cristol Springs – believe me, we checked with all the remaining dealers in six surrounding towns, and the local hospital and clinics all keep strict records with their supplies. So the good detective, that one right there, determined that Mr. Poulfry must've brought that poison with him. I know, I know, a musician with drugs! Who has ever heard of such a thing? But this man was our homegrown hero. He did more for our town and state than most of its natural attractions, so writing him off as just another tragic overdose like Hendrix or Morrison or Joplin was simply out of the question."

"Again, what does this have to do with marching us up here to negotiate the music rights for *another tragic overdose*?" Malcolm asked.

"Well, Mr. Spier, my good friend here, Detective Delijo, remembered something recently. He remembered that one of the first people to rush to Nate Poulfry's suite was one of your employees. No, it's not Ms. Rogers I'm talking about. It was Poulfry's nurse: Alexis Drison. Please don't look so confused. We are well aware that nurses don't write scripts, they simply moderate and distribute the supplies. Mr. Spier, Detective Delijo delved a bit further into what type of a doctor would prescribe a recovering addict such a potent pain medication, and he turned up the name of your private physician."

For effect, Lamprey closely scanned the largely embellished documents. He dragged his index finger over the page, pretending to search for a name that he had long before memorized. Malcolm's disposition had quickly shifted from aggravation to a witness-under-interrogation silence. He stared at the mayor with contempt, but the rest of his features could have belonged to a man sitting through a dull wedding mass.

"We contacted your long-time friend and company physician, Doctor Baylin and were able to confirm that you had personally asked him to treat Poulfry for severe pain due to his worsening arthritis. The good doctor also confirmed that you had urged him to be generous in his supplies of the painkiller because Poulfry was insistent on finishing his tour. Now, Mr. Spier, I realize that you cannot be directly held accountable for the man's death, but this type of publicity – basically ordering controlled substances for an old man so he could finish his final tour – wouldn't put your company, or your doctor's career, in the most positive of lights. In fact, after your recent activity in New Hampshire – yeah, I'm well aware of the details – I believe the investigating officers might be interested in taking another look at your account of things, especially if the Poulfry situation were ever to make its way to the media."

The final part of Lamprey's threat had not been in the script that Delijo had rehearsed. He kept his gaze fixed on Spier and Charlie Orin, and if either had been looking back at him, they would have seen the flinch of his eyebrows. As Delijo regained his composure, he felt the silence settle into the moment; it had descended from Lamprey's lips, fallen with gravity into the clearing, and was desperately looking for an escape. It seemed to encompass everyone and everything until Malcolm tore it apart. Through a clenched jaw, he spat his words and his saliva onto the confident town official.

"I won't sit here and listen to this shit! Who the hell do you think you are? You think a small-town hick of a…"

Someone grabbed his arm with a force that shocked Malcolm away from his building tirade. He turned to see Charlie Orin, a man he had known and trusted for decades, staring at him like a stranger. Malcolm ripped his arm free from the vice-like grip, but remained silent. Charlie shifted his stare to Lamprey and spoke calmly and professionally.

"Would you please give us a minute, Mr. Lamprey? As his lawyer, there are a few things I need to review with Mr. Spier."

"Take ten of them, Mr. Orin. I'm sure there is quite a bit you'd like to discuss with your client. We'll be just down the trail toward that valley if you need us."

"I can assure you, we won't need long at all."

Lamprey nodded and gestured to the detective. They walked toward the new path and were out of sight within a few steps. Malcolm glared at Charlie and took two violent steps toward his lawyer. Charlie looked up slightly to meet the stare of his boss, and spoke before Malcolm could process his thoughts into words.

"Don't fucking stare at me like I just screwed something for you, *old buddy*. Jesus Christ, Malcolm, is this worth it? Is it really worth a few grand to send us all to jail, or worse? What he's talking about, whether it's substantiated or not, is enough to bury the company and ruin the careers of dozens of hard-working people. You really want to end up in prison with me and your doctor so you can squeeze a few more dollars out of Nate Poulfry? You really want to destroy Makayla's career over this? This woman who followed your sadistic tutelage and helped bring your company out from the dregs should not lose her life and chances because you can't think clearly."

Malcolm heard what Charlie said, but didn't listen to a word of it. He didn't see reason standing in front of him – he saw weakness, and it revolted him. He focused his eyes directly on Charlie's and spoke.

"This is all – these nature walks, his theories – a load of horseshit, and if you're afraid of his fantasy threats then you're a bigger pussy than I ever thought. You really think I'll be shaken down by some rube of a mayor? Do you think that I can't handle this pissant? Do you think he's leaving here with any of our rights or property?"

Charlie closed his eyes, bent his head, and shook it four or five times. He was trying to erase Malcolm from his mind's eye as if this entire scene was unfolding on some obscene Etch-a-Sketch. Before he could organize his thoughts, Malcolm walked into him, lowering his shoulder into Charlie's and pushing him out of the way. Malcolm made his way to the edge of the small clearing and knelt for a bit more balance. He couldn't stay in his new pose for very long, so he knew his speech would have to be quick and succinct. He picked up a rock and tossed it over the edge.

"Charlie...Makayla...I'm not giving these assholes an inch, and you don't have to worry about the repercussions of my decision, because as soon as I finish this sentence, you can consider yourselves unemployed."

He heard Charlie's footsteps crunch over the dead pine needles, coming toward him, and instantly assumed that the old man was about to begin a pathetic attempt at reconciliation. He rose from his crouch, but did not turn to meet his former friend and lawyer.

"Charlie, don't even bother with trying to…"

Malcolm abruptly stopped his sentence when he felt Charlie's hands rip the collar of his shirt and the waist of his shorts backwards. Like a bouncer who's had enough of a truculent drunk, Charlie used his momentum to shove Malcolm gracefully over the precipice. Malcolm fell like a diver who had planted incorrectly on the board. His arms flailed in erratic waves, and his rising stomach and airless lungs prevented any screams from escaping his mouth. Charlie watched as Malcolm's body hit the first collection of rocks and heard him let out a terrific scream of agony after the repeated snapping of his leg. The screws and plates had held, but the bone had splintered underneath them. With each successive roll down the hill, Charlie heard Malcolm's shrieks, to his shock and dismay. Charlie didn't mind that Malcolm was suffering, but he was terrified that the impact had failed to kill him. For an instant, Charlie thought of following his victim over the edge, as he had for the last couple of years, except in this plunge he would dive head first to ensure the job was done right.

Before he could act on his thoughts, however, he saw Malcolm's body take one final roll and then pitch forward into what looked like a shallow pit. Whatever was in the pit abruptly halted Malcolm's motion and screams. Part of his body protruded from the hole while the rest lay hidden within the darkness. Before Charlie could comprehend what he was seeing, he heard Makayla cry out for Delijo's or Lamprey's help.

Charlie felt horrified and betrayed. He couldn't believe that she was calling them for help, exposing him as a murderer. He was again contemplating his waterless dive when he heard her add the words.

"Malcolm's fallen over the edge!"

Charlie ran to the path and started mimicking her

cries for help until the detective and the mayor returned. They entered in a sprint and immediately began asking, in calming, soothing voices, what the hell had happened. Makayla fell to her knees – one hell of an effect, Charlie thought – and began babbling about Malcolm throwing a fit while he had been too close to the edge of the clearing. She paused and wept and spoke and wept, and pointed Delijo to the spot of the fall. He ran to it, but slowed and crouched as he approached the edge. Like a machine, he scanned a straight path down the hill until he saw Malcolm's twisted body sticking out of a punji pit. The hole, complete with its jagged iron spikes, was the last remaining booby trap of the area. Malcolm's body had found what Delijo and his team had missed.

Delijo immediately turned and ran down the path that led to the valley floor. It would take at least three minutes to get to the body, but regardless of the odds against Malcolm being alive, Delijo ran as fast as the terrain would allow. He lost his footing only once, quickly recovered himself, and continued his race against time. As he approached the pit, he slowed down and began scanning the ground for abnormalities. Many booby traps would be set close together, ready to ensnare those remaining souls who thought themselves safe. The ground appeared to be solid between Malcolm and himself, so Delijo picked up his pace until he was standing over the corpse. Of the four spikes sticking through Malcolm, Delijo figured, without much trouble, that the one protruding through his forehead had been the lucky winner in this most deadly game. The blood had engulfed one of Malcolm Spier's eyes, and the other stared blankly into the sky. Delijo turned and looked upwards to see the others staring down at him. He paused briefly and then shook his head.

XXIII

Charlie, Makayla, and Alexis sat around the small dining table in their plush hotel suite, dining on a sumptuous meal as the late evening light showered through the window panes and terrace double-doors. Andrew Lamprey had graciously extended their stay in Cristol Springs so they could finish both their police and professional business arrangements. Without objections, they had moved into their new rooms, and had decided to take complete advantage of the complimentary perks. Three days had passed since Malcolm's death, and his absence seemed to liberate the remaining upper tier of SR&E. His latent malevolent presence was quickly dissipating with the season's waning light, and their discussions revolved around the possibilities that Malcolm's impaled skull had opened. None of these ideas were professed with much gusto, though, seeing how neither Charlie nor Makayla wished to be associated with the label any longer.

Perhaps falsely, trying to rationalize the fact that they had murdered their boss, or perhaps authentically, accepting that someone like Malcolm Spier could not be allowed to live, they ate and conversed with seemingly guiltless consciences. When they had finished discussing the potential benefits that Malcolm's death could berth, they finally decided to recount the details to Alexis. Up to this point, Makayla had not explained the specifics, yet now she and Charlie indulged her with every grisly detail. They explained to her how Lamprey had exposed Malcolm as a fraud at best and a murderer at worst; they explained how Malcolm had reacted, and how Charlie had decided to end this obscene charade; they recounted his fall, his roll down the cliff, and his dive onto the spears. Finally, they told her how they had played off one another, and how both Lamprey and Delijo had accepted their story without many questions at all.

"They were probably as happy as we were to be rid of him," Charlie said, finishing his last bit of steak. "More than likely they heard what they wanted to hear."

Makayla twirled the final flake of salmon back and forth through the creamy sauce, paused, looked up at Charlie, and asked him why he'd done it.

"That man was sick, Mackie, and he needed to be stopped. I'm not saying I'm a champion of morality or justice – far from it, in fact – but I realized that he had gone beyond the point of recognizing the consequences that his bullshit would have on others, and therefore beyond the point of being able to discern enemies from friends. I'd known Malcolm Spier for over forty years, and the man I threw off that ledge was not him. That person was dangerous to the people who worked with him, the people who cared for him, and the few people who loved him."

He held an exaggerated pause, twirled the wine in his glass, drank most of it, and smiled.

"Besides, I've been screwing his wife for close to three years now, and I could not risk him finding out."

Makayla dropped her fork and stared at Charlie Orin. He looked only to his Chardonnay.

"How the hell could he not know that?" she asked incredulously.

"Simple. He hadn't given a thought to her or any of her needs in a long time. She and I grew closer as he disappeared. We fell in love, and she left him just as all of this was starting. I love her, I truly do, but as much as

I care for her, I still felt guilty about betraying him. After she left him, I tried to see if he would save his own damn marriage by encouraging him to go after her, but he refused. He didn't care about her while she was around, didn't even care about her enough to file for a divorce. For him, she was out of sight, out of mind. He couldn't use her for anything, so he had no need for her. All this time, she was a few towns over with me. I didn't think it would be hard to figure out, though, so after he came back from New Hampshire, I decided that Claire and I needed to get away from him. If he were capable of killing his own nephew, he wouldn't have thought twice about butchering the two of us. When I saw the opportunity on our recent nature walk, I took it."

Makayla was staring at Charlie, and she was sure that Alexis was too. She poured some more wine for herself and Alexis and let the silence linger.

"So what the hell happens to the company?" Alexis asked.

"Well, that's an interesting query. As fastidious as he was, Malcolm never bothered to update his will or his life insurance policy. Everything that was Malcolm's is now Claire's, and I can assure you she wants nothing to do with the record business. I called her the afternoon he died to tell her what had happened. As Malcolm's attorney, and boyfriend of the widow, I can assure you that I, too, want nothing to do with this business. We're going to take what's left and get the hell away. What happens to the company does not have to be decided right now, but someone will either have to take the reins or we'll have to start selling off what's left of the rights and materials. Makayla, as the company's legal authority, I want to offer you the opportunity to become the sole proprietor of SR&E. I imagine that, if you accept, you'd want to get rid of the name."

Makayla stared at Charlie and contemplated his proposition. Alexis slid her hand under the table and placed it over her lover's rigid fingers. Feeling its soothing encouragement, Makayla let her entire body relax as she returned the tender embrace. Only days prior to this dinner, Makayla Rogers had wanted to separate herself physically and emotionally from Malcolm Spier, but she did not completely want to remove herself from what she'd learned and experienced while under his guidance. Discovering her direction had taken exhausting years, yet in such a short amount of time she had grown into her producer role. Now she needed to know what it might be like to cultivate musicians' talents legitimately. Charlie, always the astute negotiator, read the dilemma on her face, put his wine down, and tried to reassure her.

"I couldn't think of a better person to take the lead of SR&E than you, Ms. Rogers, but I want you to think very carefully about what being in control might do to you...and to her," he added, nodding toward Alexis. "Malcolm, as best as I can remember, never spoke of wanting to harm anyone or anything until the world he'd grown accustomed to was ripped away from him. He had been able to deal with loss – anyone who's been in this long enough can – but the losses were always measured against the victories in a game he was familiar with. When the entire industry fell apart, Malcolm didn't know – shit, none of us knew – how to adapt. The new type of fans are demanding, whether they realize it or not, an entirely unfeasible way to produce music. I still can't figure out how they expect new artists to flourish when they only buy one or two tracks on a whim or subscribe to Internet radio sites. Now you might be sharp enough to realize that this phase will pass and another change in the game will come, but I want you to realize that when it does, you'll either be at the forefront of it or you'll be able to leave with your dignity and a little bit of money. I want you to be able to make your exit on your own terms, and not at the hands of your most trusted friend. I'm sorry for the lecture, but I want you to think very carefully about where you'd take this company before you give me an answer. I need to be sure that Malcolm's methods ended with him."

Charlie sat back, proud yet slightly embarrassed by his sermon. He expected to excuse himself from the table without further discussion, but Makayla surprised his loosely planned exit.

"I want it, Charlie, but I want everything associated with him gone. I also need you to help me in the transition, and after it's over, we will part our ways graciously."

He was a bit taken aback that she hadn't matched his tirade with one of her own, but he accepted her terse response.

"There's no rush. We'll work out those details when we get back to New York. For now, let's enjoy some dessert and the evening. Tomorrow we'll grant Mr. Lamprey whatever he desires from our Poulfry collection and leave."

XXIV

In the year that followed Spier's death, Charlie had the title and rights of the company turned over, with Claire Spier's blessings, to Makayla Rogers. Before the transfer was complete, Makayla, Charlie, and many of the devastated employees planned a small tribute show for the late record executive. To Makayla's dismay, a surprising tally of his past and current clients arrived and performed. Had they known what Malcolm had been planning for them, they probably would have watched from the comforts of their own homes, but the lure of the stage and the audience and the cameras was too powerful to resist. While the show would only have a fraction of the exposure that Pearle Collier's had had, the New Hampshire scandal was still fresh enough in the public's psyche to generate a modest return. The show, hosted in a small venue, quickly sold out, mainly to other labels that were looking to poach some new clients, but Makayla wasn't concerned. She was going to take her new label in an entirely new direction, so if they wanted a few has-beens or Everett Beechum's latest group, they were welcome to them.

One of the final aspects of SR&E that Charlie had reviewed with her had actually been Beechum's quarterly numbers. They were very impressive. His aunt's death had finally exposed him to the public's awareness, and his talent, as he always knew it could, had been able to sustain a moderate fame. Makayla was very pleased to learn that his worth had drastically increased because she was more than willing to terminate his contract and liberate him. She had not had any direct contact with him – he had absolutely refused to speak or meet with her after what her father had done – and he was more than willing to sacrifice his royalties and album rights in order to be free. He had also refused to play Malcolm's tribute show until Charlie informed him of the labels that would be in attendance.

When the music, speeches, and entertainment had wrapped, Makayla came to the stage to pay a final tribute to the memory of Malcolm Spier. She was seething inside, disgusted by the applause that Malcolm's enlarged portrait received, but she maintained her smile, never letting any of this nostalgic nonsense replace the memories of the man he had actually been. She waved to some of Poulfry's fans, and reveled in the fact that Malcolm's miserable life and poetic death were going to jump start her new company. She gave a short speech in which she honored his contributions to the music industry, invited the remaining SR&E staff onto the stage, and finally led them in a bow and a thank you to the fans.

Makayla then conducted some brief post-show interviews and met with the pop producer and talent scout from Titular Records, Alan Scithe. They had begun their preliminary hearings for Beechum's career, and within weeks they had signed and sealed his new contract. After Everett Beechum's release, the company began to shed employees, artists, and office space. Eventually, as Makayla had intended after leaving Cristol Springs, there were no physical remnants of SR&E.

Makayla and Alexis had decided that New York was the poisoned realm of Spier. They had all agreed, even Charlie, that the old offices and town should be left to recover from Malcolm's corruption without their assistance. They did not want to salvage anything; they wanted to move on. Neither Makayla nor Alexis knew exactly where to go, but the Empire State had offered all it could in damaged memories and gilded opportunities.

Makayla was easily settling into her new town. Bastion, Texas was actually on the cusp of the indie rock scene, and it seemed to attract youth and vitality from all over the country. Artists of all genres, chefs of all styles, and entrepreneurs with profound and wide-ranging ideas flocked to the downtown area and created a modern community. Makayla and Alexis felt as if they had been vacationing in other states and cities for the better parts of their lives, and they had now finally, thankfully, returned home. Alexis had quickly found a job in the local hospital, and Makayla had worked tirelessly to establish her new label, Themis Records. She focused her advertisements on the LGBT community and proposed generous and encouraging incentives to play at her small festivals. She produced many of these shows in order to attract talented bands that would be largely overlooked by pop labels, constantly auditioning groups and working late into the nights. Her reputation of being a relaxed, reasonable professional began to spread. While she was not making much money, she felt fulfilled and truly happy.

It was after a long night of drinking and judging talent that she noticed the alert on her phone from *celebdirrt.com*. She looked down in horror at its words: *Rising star and horn virtuoso Everett Beechum found dead from drug overdose.* She clicked on the link and read the full article. When she finished it, she scrolled back up to scour the details she'd already forgotten. She could not imagine that Beechum would have thrown away his rising career for a needle. When she had worked with him and Pearle Collier, he had abstained from everything except some celebratory glasses of champagne. She scrolled back down and read the small paragraph that outlined some minor substance abuse issues he had had in his teenage years. No matter where she scrolled or what she searched, she couldn't make sense of his death. According to Charlie, Beechum had been much more vocal about his shares in the final negotiations between SR&E and Titular, but his opinions, suggestions, and objections had been made lucidly and professionally. When Makayla had seen him perform at Malcolm's show, she had noticed that fame had been agreeing with him; he had looked fit, lithe, and prepared to entertain for decades to come.

She put her phone down and began to tremble. Spier was dead, she had witnessed that with her own eyes, but this news seemed to be ominously familiar to her. She picked up her phone and called Alexis. She didn't expect to reach her during the night shift, but she needed to try. The call immediately went to voicemail.

"Call me when you can," she whimpered.

Makayla's tremors increased as the feelings of isolation flooded back into her; she hadn't felt this vulnerable in months. She needed to escape, but there was nowhere for her to retreat. She picked her phone back up and began searching for other articles about Everett Beechum. One title froze her finger to the screen. It read: *Everett Beechum, Newest Member of the Seemingly Cursed Titular Records, Found Dead.*

"Why cursed?" she whispered to the phone.

She tapped on the link which sent her to the answer. The connection she found would have been purely coincidental to an average music fan, but to Makayla it was terrifyingly deliberate. According to the blog, Titular Records had lost one of its other prominent artists, Ms. Rita Symone, several years earlier to a tragic accident involving a mélange of drugs and an oversized pleasure toy. Makayla continued reading, learning that Titular had made a fortune off of Symone's death. Suddenly, violently, Makayla hurled the phone against the wall of her office. Beechum's death was no more an accident than Symone's had been. She screamed at herself; she cursed Malcolm. She fell back into her seat, realizing that she had handed Beechum over to a company that had figured out SR&E's method long before her old, twisted boss.

Letting her arms fall to her side, Makayla stared blankly out into the Texas night.